WAY OF THE CANYON

WAY OF THE CANYON

By
Victoria Lourdes Medina Baker

XULON ELITE

Xulon Press Elite
555 Winderley Pl, Suite 225
Maitland, FL 32751
407.339.4217
www.xulonpress.com

Paperback ISBN-13: 979-8-86850-877-6
Ebook ISBN-13: 979-8-86850-878-3

DEDICATION

I dedicate this book to my dear husband, Vernon Baker, loving sons, Jeremy Baker and Christopher Baker, and darling daughter, Vanessa (Baker) McKay. Since the day each of you entered my life, my heart has swelled with a love I can never put into words.

ACKNOWLEDGEMENTS

Once again, thank you to "*You and I Creative Co.*" https://www.youandicreate.co/ Vanessa and Levi McKay, for another breathtaking cover design. Your designs never fail to be just what I hope for (and more). The Canyon continues thriving, not only through the words of this book, but through your inspiring talent that blows me away, every single time.

To my family which has grown from 5 to 12+ of us over the years, thank you, each one of you, for encouraging and inspiring me, even when you don't realize you have. All our phone calls, texts and messages keep us close to each other. I look forward to many more memories, whether we gather in our beloved Canyon, or places near and far, my favorite time ever is spending it with you all.

Vernon, you continue being the diamond of my heart. Thank you for reading, editing and sharing your input with this second book. It helped more than you know.

Jeremy, Eden, Jaycee and Elyn, you continue being the gems of my heart. Jaycee and Elyn, you will always be my beautiful princesses. I love sharing life and experiences with all of you.

Christopher, Paige and Alexis, you continue being the gems of my heart. Alexis, you are beautiful inside and out. I am honored to call you one of my grand girls! Chris, thank you for reading, editing and all your passion and creative input with this second book. You helped so very much!

Vanessa, Levi, Oakley (and the 3 boys) you continue being the gems of my heart. Oakley, you are perfectly perfect in every way, and so very adorable! Nessa, thank you for being so real with your editing and input with this second book. Your help is always invaluable.

Each of you inspire me and make me glow every single day. I love you more than words.

TABLE OF CONTENTS

1. Life Goes On 1
2. Still Around 5
3. Sunday Family Meal 9
4. Staying Focused. 13
5. Canyon Time 15
6. Opening Up 19
7. Izrael's Plan 23
8. Dreamy Days 27
9. Journal Escapes 31
10. Cherry Pies. 35
11. Meal Chatter 39
12. Momma's Girls 43
13. Interruptions 47
14. Seeing Clearly 51
15. What's Next? 55
16. Secrets of the Orchard 59
17. Attending Church 65
18. The Sunday Lunch 69
19. Back to the Plan 75
20. Hard Memories 79
21. Getting Clarity 83
22. Pieces of Pie. 87
23. Momma Knows Best 91

24. Unveiling of Wisdom 95
25. Encounters and Questions 99
26. The Reverend's Visit 105
27. More Questions 111
28. Carolina Opens Up 113
29. Taking a Stand 119
30. Men Talk 123
31. Disbelief 127
32. The Real Story 131
33. Tuesday's Coming 135
34. Once a Liar Always a Liar 137
35. Let's Take a Break 143
36. Church Gossip 145
37. A Critical Visit 149
38. Restless Waiting 155
39. Jane Mae 161
40. Momma's New Thoughts 163
41. Izrael's Friends 165
42. Relief or Not? 169
43. Izrael 171
44. Traveling 175
45. Time Well Spent 179
46. Welcome Home 183
47. What Plans? 187
48. Now What? 195
49. Fixing Things 199
50. Small Glimpses 203
51. Baby Briella 207
52. The Real Father 213
53. Dear Grandma K 219
54. Shining in the Distance 223

PROLOGUE

"Where did my name come from, Grandma Jane Mae?" Marcus often asked his grandma when he was a young child. Over the years he never received a straight answer.

As Marcus Parker, now a grown man, pondered conversations from the past, his mind quickly moved from the past to his present and continual obsession. He was more prepared than ever to begin phase one of his plan. His business had become much more lucrative. He could afford to buy whatever he wanted. He wanted Kammer Ranch more than ever, but it was not for sale. Money was not part of phase one.

Jane Mae Parker's grandson, Marcus Parker, had not given up planning to take over Kammer Ranch. So far, he was unable to find the shiny object he had spotted glimmering against the sunlight several years past. He could not shake off feeling that the object was key to his success. He had to find it and he WOULD find it, he told himself often.

The vastness of the land, Marcus believed, could work to his advantage. The stories Grandma Jane Mae Parker shared with him; of living in a small camper deep in Kammer land inspired and intrigued him. Phase one included Marcus sneaking onto the property to look around for his hiding place. He knew better than to drive into the canyon, for fear of being caught. Instead, Marcus planned to backpack in and stay for long stretches of time. His priority, to find the shiny object.

The time was coming soon. He could feel it. One day, it would all be his. ONLY his. One day.

INTRODUCTION

Over the last several years, Kammer Ranch continued thriving. The valley was as beautiful as ever, with the deep greens and bright yellows that filled the view in almost every direction. The peace that echoed through the trees bowed down only to the sounds of the woodpeckers. They were tapping, tapping so persistently, as if to say, "Let me in, you know I'm not going anywhere, you might as well let me in!"

The woodpeckers' persistence reminded Izrael Shane Kammer every day of the persistency of someone from his past who also would not go away. No matter what he did, Carolina Jane Parker was always close by, always tapping, tapping, so persistently, saying, "Let us in, you know we're not going anywhere, you might as well let us in!"

Each year, in early autumn, the valley filled with yellow wildflowers and sunflowers. Travelers often stopped along the main roads to take pictures of the sprawling colors that mixed with a soft sage green, resembling pillows, for the flowers to lay their heads to rest overnight. In the morning they were vibrant again, reaching their glowing faces towards the sun, begging for warmth. The sun happily reached down to add to their magnificence. The families in the valley loved this time of year. Mommas of young children kept jars with fresh water on their kitchen tables. Their children filled the jars with wildflowers nearly every day. Even if the flowers made those mommas sneeze, they fussed and thanked their precious ones for the beautiful bouquets.

Izrael's younger sisters continued the same tradition each year, gathering the biggest and brightest flowers they could find. There would occasionally be a purple or pink flower in the mix which was always a delight to Suzanah Grace Klein Kammer. She made sure to show surprise at the beauty of the flowers her girls, Josephina, and Nikola, brought to her. "What a beautiful time of year!" she would exclaim as she hugged and kissed each girl, holding them close, treasuring every moment. Suzanah had learned how quickly life changes; soon her younger girls would be women. Her two older daughters, Lucy and Priscilla were now married women. Izrael, her only son, was now a man. His decisions in life would bring more changes to the family, Suzanah was sure. As good momma's do, she pondered and prayed daily for each in her family, including her loving husband Alexander Shane Kammer (Alex K). How would the changes impact him, she thought quietly to herself. She pulled her shawl in tightly around her shoulders as she felt the cool breeze around her. Cooler days and nights were soon to come. So much more was ahead for the Kammer family. As the impending arrival of fall and winter weather, change would soon be upon them.

CHAPTER 1

"LIFE GOES ON"

Izrael continued to work with Poppa, Alex K, who had grown more and more dependent on his son over the years. They worked the ranch together day to day with occasional outings for supplies and such. Things were going well on Kammer Ranch. There had been growth, buying additional land and adding more cattle, selling of cattle and horses, and renting land to other families. Some of the rancher families in the valley needed to rent space for their cattle or horses to graze. Many ranchers in the area were jealous of Kammer Ranch and its beauty. Alex K saw them as being lazy. He felt if he and his son could create such a beautiful and healthy ranch, why couldn't they? It irritated him but he also knew the income from renting would benefit him and his beautiful wife, Suzanah one day. Alex K chose to open a savings account with the money from renting out grazing. Suzanah thought Alex K was over cautious, but she trusted him more than anyone and never argued those types of things with him.

Now that Izrael's older sisters, Lucy, and Priscilla (Cilla) were both married, Iz was determined to make time to visit with them. Lucy had a baby recently. Izrael could hardly believe he was an uncle. He loved being an uncle. He would often ride his beloved Mindee over to visit Lucy and the baby. Lucy and her husband, Frank Cleveland, lived north of Kammer Ranch and deep into another canyon.

Priscilla married a young man named Mark Samson, from another ranch. They lived on the Samson family property, as Mark worked the ranch with his father. This was a common pattern for the families in the valleys, as daughters married rancher sons and carried on traditions that lingered and were greatly loved by the people of the valley. Samson Ranch was close to Kammer Ranch. In fact, they could walk back and forth, through a gate made of barbed wire fencing, to visit and they did so often. The homes were divided by "Momma's Orchard" as the family referred to all the fruit trees Momma had planted over the years.

Iz and his sisters never really noticed all the work Momma put into her orchard when they were younger. The orchard was filled with apple trees that produced smaller green, more sour apples Momma used for baking delicious apple pies. Momma also planted plum trees and choke cherry trees. The choke cherry was popular in the valley, as they were small trees which made it easy to pick the fruit and made for a tasty jam. It wasn't Momma's favorite, but she knew the rest of the family liked it. She always kept a well-stocked pantry of choke cherry jam. The small jars made the perfect gift for unexpected guests or new families moving into the valley. Momma had several cherry trees in the orchard, but none compared to the beautiful tree off the front porch of the ranch house. Wild birds took over the very top of the tree. Momma always said God intended those cherries for them, and not for human consumption. Momma's famous cherry pie was still a favorite for the family, especially when the cherries came from the big tree and not from the orchard.

Neighbors continued to "happen by" when the cherries from the big tree were ready for picking. Many people in the valley said there was no other tree like it. Izrael believed it too. He loved when all the families came over to fill their buckets alongside the Kammer, Cleveland and Samson families. It was a very special day for everyone involved.

Izrael found it strange to not have Lucy and Cilla around the Kammer Ranch house every day, helping Momma and teasing him constantly. He missed them both being there daily, but the family remained close. Iz often stated he would do whatever it takes to keep it that way. Izrael had said this out loud enough times that it concerned Momma a little, but she kept those thoughts to herself, knowing he would talk if he needed to, as always.

CHAPTER 2

"STILL AROUND"

Grandpa K's tractors still sit proudly on Kammer Ranch. Long ago used, long ago (almost) forgotten. Izrael had faint memories of Grandpa K running the tractor across the lower fields for growing vegetables. He also remembered some of the words Grandpa K yelled when the tractor stopped running. Grandpa K used to make lists of parts he needed for his tractor, then count coins from the money allotted for repairs. He was often heard saying some of the same words, while counting, that he had yelled outside. Izrael understood more now, why that was such a big deal to Grandpa K. Izrael felt a sad ache in his heart as he thought of Grandpa K, and all the wonderful lessons he taught Iz. Those lessons helped to form him into the man he was now. This gave Izrael a brief feeling of hope to one day have children and grandchildren. He would pass the same lessons on to them. In his thoughts he resolved to make an entry in his journal later that evening.

His thoughts were suddenly and abruptly interrupted by the sound of a horn. Iz knew that sound could only be one person, and he was right. Carolina Parker sat in the driver's seat waving her arm out the window as if Izrael could not see her large and ugly brown car. A fainter sound emitted from the back seat where Jane Mae always sat. She had grown a lot over the past few years.

Jane Mae was now 7 years old, going on about 20, based on her current mood. Iz did not feel up to dealing with whichever mood was happening at the moment. Even worse, he did not want to talk with Carolina. Normally he was able to avoid these kinds of moments, but today he could not duck out of sight. They had already spotted him on the porch while loudly yelling greetings out the windows of the ugly brown car. "What do you need, Carolina? I'm busy," Iz flatly asked Carolina as she pulled forward in the long, curved driveway.

"Well, that's not too friendly of a greeting, Izrael Shane Kammer, what's the matter?" Carolina responded in an eerily pouty voice. Iz rolled his eyes and said a short hello to Jane Mae as she hopped out of the back seat. Jane Mae took off towards the old playhouse Suzanah's father had built after Lucy was born. Jane Mae seemed to think it had been hers only. No one bothered to tell Carolina, nor Jane Mae, where it came from. "At least she stays out of trouble," Iz blurted out.

"What was that?" Carolina answered as she walked over towards the porch. "Nothing, I was just thinking I need to check on Mindee, and be sure she hasn't gotten into any trouble," Izrael said quickly as he scurried past Carolina towards the barn area where Mindee grazed most days.

Carolina spent most of her days doing odd jobs around the valley, making just enough money to get by. Her mother would stay home with Jane Mae while Carolina worked. Suzanah, too, had given Carolina a little work here and there when she could spare some money.

Today Carolina's mother was not feeling too well so Jane Mae tagged along while Carolina worked cleaning out Suzanah's pantry. It was almost time for canning vegetables and fruit that had been collected from the garden. Suzanah, Lucy and Priscilla still got together to do the canning in preparation for the winter. In order to be ready for the week of canning, Suzanah needed to prepare the pantry.

"Hello! Is anyone in here? Hello!" Carolina screeched through the slightly open window. Suzanah jumped when she heard Carolina, trying hard to keep her thoughts neutral.

"Come in, Carolina, come on in," Suzanah greeted Carolina quickly. "I can only stay a couple of hours, Ms. Kammer. Jane Mae is with me today. She's playing in her playhouse."

"Her playhouse?" Suzanah thought to herself. "It's not her playhouse!" She wanted to blurt out but kept her thoughts quiet.

"We can do a lot in a couple of hours," Suzanah replied, forcing a small smile. Suzanah normally felt uneasy with Carolina, but she knew giving Carolina a little work helped her with the expenses of raising a child. They began silently removing jars and other items from the pantry in order to scrub the shelves. Not many words were spoken while they cleaned. An occasional sneeze followed by, "God bless you" kept the silence from crowding the space.

About an hour into their work, the screen door squeaked and slammed loudly against the side of the kitchen table. The whiney squawk quickly followed, "Mommy!! I'm hungry!!!" Suzanah flinched and nearly dropped the bucket of cleaning solution she had carried back from the kitchen sink. "Mommy!! I said I'm hungry, can't you hear anything?!!" Jane Mae screeched towards Carolina.

"Can't you see I'm busy, child? Go back outside and play!!"

"I don't want to play outside, there's nothing to do and I'm hungry, Mommy!!"

Suzanah stepped towards the kitchen table and invited Jane Mae to have a biscuit with jam. Jane Mae smiled and happily sat down. She quickly devoured the biscuit, wiped her mouth with her sleeve then crumpled the napkin Suzanah had placed next to her plate. Licking her fingers and talking with biscuit crumbs falling from her mouth, Jane Mae yelled out, "I'm going outside Mommy!"

Carolina barely gave any attention to Jane Mae. Suzanah felt sad watching the two interacting with each other. This brought back memories and emotions for Suzanah. She loved her own children deeply. She would never have treated them the way Carolina treated Jane Mae. She also knew her children would never have yelled at her the way Jane Mae yelled at Carolina. Suzanah prayed to herself for a softness between them, feeling close to tears as she watched their exchange with each other.

Izrael was working near enough by the house to hear the screeching voice of Jane Mae when she entered the house and later when she ran back outside. He found himself, again, shaking his head, wondering why Momma let Carolina do jobs for her. He knew how good Momma was, and how she could never turn away anyone in need. Not even Carolina and Jane Mae. Again, he shook his head and went back to cleaning the stalls and raking back the dirt around the barn. He felt happy, a little later, when he heard the engine of the old brown car start up, knowing the two were leaving. Izrael longed for the final time they would leave Kammer Ranch.

"One day," Izrael spoke softly to himself, "One day."

CHAPTER 3

"SUNDAY FAMILY MEAL"

Sunday meals continued to be special for the Kammer family. While they had their own homes, both Lucy and Priscilla, along with their husbands and Lucy's baby would gather at Kammer Ranch for their weekly family meal. Lucy and Priscilla prepared and brought part of the meal to add to what Momma prepared. Most meals consisted of a meat such as chicken, beef or pork, potatoes, vegetables, biscuits and of course, Momma's cherry pie. Lucy's baby, Briella Suzanah, was too young for table food and was not sitting up yet. Briella was a calm, sweet baby and so very endearing that she was quite the distraction for everyone working in the kitchen.

Momma, especially, would rush to the bassinet where Briella lay quietly making soft baby sounds, just to coo and giggle with her. "Oh, Momma," Lucy said smiling, "You're going to spoil my baby!"

"That's the point, my dear Lucy, that's the point," Momma answered in a sweet voice meant only for Briella. Briella Suzanah happily cooed back to Momma and squealed with delight." As Momma stepped back to the counter where she had been chopping vegetables, she stopped to squeeze Lucy's hand and say, "I am still so pleased with her name, Lucy, thank you for such an honor."

"Momma, it's fine, you don't have to thank me every time we see each other," Lucy answered. The two laughed quietly while Priscilla and the two younger girls continued preparing the meal.

Everyone nearly jumped when Briella let out a loud squeal of delight, knowing even before turning to see Izrael leaning in talking quietly with the baby. Briella loved her "Uncle Iz" as Lucy fondly referred to her baby brother for Briella's sake. Izrael's two younger sisters, Josephina and Nikola could not resist running over to be at each side of Iz while they joined in admiring their beautiful niece.

Izrael loved Briella just as much, if not more than she loved him. He loved the shape of her face, her little nose that crinkled up slightly when she laughed, and the endearing sound of her voice. Briella was blessed with dark curly hair so shiny the sunlight reflected off her curls. "How can one baby be so perfect?" Izrael said loud enough for the family to hear him. Everyone smiled in agreement, except Lucy. Lucy felt a sense of fear for having such a perfectly beautiful child. She feared another child from their past would cause problems. She felt an air of jealousy from that child was somehow eerily hovering over Briella. Thankfully their paths had not yet crossed, but even these thoughts made Lucy uneasy. She was sure the rest of the family had the same thoughts, though no one dared speak it, for fear of what it might bring.

Most families in the valley did not take their new babies out except to extended family until the baby was at least 3 months old. Lucy felt very protective of Briella. The last time a baby had been in the Kammer family home was when Carolina had taken Jane Mae over insisting Izrael was the baby's father.

Lucy's thoughts were interrupted when Poppa entered the kitchen, and the family began to sit around the table. An uneasy quiet settled in the room, like a dark cloud pinned onto their shoulders. The platters of food passed from hand to hand, in a slow steady rhythm that nearly resembled a funeral song.

"What was this thick feeling of gloom?" Izrael thought to himself. Suddenly he felt it was his responsibility to figure it out. The determination felt strong, and Izrael would soon begin to plan.

Later in the evening, when everyone had gone to bed, Izrael pulled out his journal to make notes of what he felt earlier. The notes were followed by an outline that would be the beginning of his plans to destroy the cloud of gloom and bring joy back into the family.

CHAPTER 4

"STAYING FOCUSED"

The next day began with the usual routine. Girls in and out of the bathroom, hurrying around to not be late for school. Izrael normally attempted to be up well before his little sisters, to avoid the bathroom chaos. Today he had not awoken as early as usual. He was sure his staying awake late with his journal notes did not help him.

He hurried through his turn, into the kitchen to eat as fast as Momma would let him, then out the door to find Poppa and get busy with their workday. Poppa was not too far ahead and Iz hurried his pace when he saw Poppa near the corral.

"We have some work to do on these posts, son," Poppa started before Izrael reached the corral. Thankfully Iz heard what Poppa said, otherwise Poppa might get annoyed having to repeat himself.

"Yes, sir, I see that. Looks like the wood has started to rot out," Iz responded to Poppa, reaching out to touch and inspect the post Poppa had been holding. "I'll get right on it, right away, sir!" Izrael jumped into his work. There wasn't anything Izrael would not do on Kammer Ranch. Everything appealed to Iz. He felt pride and fulfillment with his work, being a real cowboy and spending his days with Poppa.

The two continued working throughout the morning, stopping now and then to go back over what they had completed. Poppa added, "This time of year we have to be extra cautious with the wood posts, son. They can rot out from one day to the next. I'd like you to keep a close eye on these around the corral, over the next few weeks. We can get back to working on them if anything starts showing signs of rotting."

"Yes, sir, Poppa! I will take charge and keep a close eye on the corral posts," Iz answered enthusiastically. This was the first time Poppa had given Iz a specific project to be in charge of. Izrael would not disappoint Poppa.

The day flew by and as they prepared to take their lunch break, Izrael remembered his personal project he had taken on the night before. He had an urge to pull out his journal and remind himself of the first steps he had written down. Iz resisted the urge. He did not want Poppa to wonder what he was writing or focusing his attention on. During the workday, there was not much room for distraction and Izrael knew better than to create any kind of issue between himself and Poppa. His goal was to keep focused, to grow as a cowboy/rancher and to not disappoint Poppa, no matter what.

Right before lunch, Iz made time to check on Mindee and her water trough. Mindee always let out her happy neigh the minute Izrael turned toward her. It was one of life's simple pleasures for Iz. He lingered just a few minutes to run his hand over Mindee's side and nuzzle into her. The two would take a ride later in the day, as they did most days, into the canyon for their end of the day escape. Izrael knew he would have time then to journal and think more about his project.

CHAPTER 5

"CANYON TIME"

Izrael had spent many, many hours in the canyon with Mindee. Today felt a little bit different, and he wasn't sure why. He just knew he needed time. The two rode for a long while, circling back here and there until finally settling at the highest open spot on the ranch. Izrael stayed on Mindee for several minutes simply staring out at the views. So many hills, rolling and rolling until one could see no further. It was breathtaking. Mindee continued to move slowly until Iz finally said, "Woah, girl, let's stop here." He threw his right leg backwards and around to meet his left leg then smoothly swept down Mindee's side. Iz patted her firmly which Mindee knew meant she could wander around close by. Mindee never strayed far. Often the two would look up at the same time, make eye contact and go back to what they were each doing. It was a strong feeling of comfort for both of them, knowing they were always there for each other. An unspoken comfort.

Iz went straight to his knapsack and pulled out his journal. He had journaled many times throughout the years since high school. Each time he wrote he remembered Grandpa K fondly. He thought about the first time he held Grandpa K's journal, remembering the hard leather and how difficult it had been to dig it out of the cold ground. Mostly he pondered on the words he read. Some had not made sense, not until he visited with Grandpa K and learned more about his past.

Iz stood staring at his pages, as he often did when he journaled. He wondered if anyone would read his words and if they might wonder what in the world his words meant. Izrael held a brief thought about what he would do with his journal. Should he hide it in the ground, as Grandpa K did? He was not sure how he felt about it being found.

His thoughts moved to the night before. Iz had written an outline on the first page. As he read over the outline, the words seemed to float from side to side and backwards and forwards, like a whirlwind of thoughts with no place to land. It was confusing Izrael and even made him a little nauseous.

At one point Izrael thought he had seen the name, "Carolina" and he almost yelled out. He stopped staring at the page, set down the journal and settled onto a large boulder placed conveniently near tall pine trees that warmly invited him into their perfect shade. Izrael gave himself time to look around at the scenery again. He wondered out loud this time, "Why would I even think of her right now?"

Iz worried that the confusion he felt would not stop. He was not sure what he would need to do to change his focus. He just knew something was unsettling and he did not like the feeling he was having.

Izrael stopped to pray, as he was accustomed to doing before writing. He realized the chaos had a lot to do with not yet praying. When he opened his eyes, he watched a small squirrel scramble to a nearby tree trunk and quickly up the tree. At that moment Izrael felt peace and calm and began to write. Iz loved moments like this. It was as if someone else was carrying his hand and gracefully crafting words that seemed to place themselves onto the pages magically. He knew it was God guiding his hand and putting the thoughts into his head. Izrael felt sure he could never do this kind of writing on his own, and he was thankful.

Time seemed to stand still. Suddenly Iz heard the faint sound of a bell. He knew that sound. Iz jumped to his feet to pack his things back into his knapsack and look around for Mindee. She was, of course, nearby. Once she heard the shuffling sounds Izrael was making, she scurried over to wait for him.

Izrael was surprised how much time had passed. He had not noticed the sun was setting and causing shadows. It would be dark soon in the canyon. He rushed to jump on Mindee's back and the two quickly took off, out of the canyon towards the house. Izrael's mind was racing almost as quickly as Mindee was galloping, over what he had written in his journal. It was a lot to think about. He was sure he knew what was bothering the family, but he needed more time to work on a plan. He hoped he would have time to journal after dinner.

As soon as Momma saw Izrael reach the first turn, coming out of the canyon, she returned to the kitchen to finish preparing dinner. Josephina and Nikola were working away, happily chatting, and getting plates out, gently laying out the cloth napkins and placing the utensils for each family member to use.

Momma smiled as she watched her younger girls. They had matured so much in the last couple of years, and they were the happiest helpers in the kitchen.

Dinner was wonderful and delicious, as usual.

CHAPTER 6

"OPENING UP"

The weather had continued to change and with the cool air came more beautiful fall colors.

No one loved the fall more than Suzanah. As soon as she first noticed the colors, she knew the weather would be nearly perfect. Suzanah would grab her latest project, whether it was writing a note to someone, writing a poem, or knitting baby booties for the newest baby in the valley, and head to the front porch. The perfect weather made for the best setting to work on her projects.

On this particular afternoon, just as Suzanah settled into her favorite chair on the porch, a lovely fall rain shower began. Suzanah smiled to herself. She then heard a car pulling up into the driveway. Suzanah stood and stretched her neck to see the back bumper and realized it was Lucy and Frank. She let out a sound of delight, knowing her beautiful granddaughter, Briella, would be with them. Suzanah set down her project and went back into the house to grab a couple of umbrellas.

By the time she stepped back out onto the porch, Frank was carrying his own umbrella which he held delicately over Lucy and their precious baby.

"Oh, come inside quickly and dry off," Momma sang out. She was so happy to see the little family but wondered why they had come over in the middle of the day. At this time-of-day Frank was usually busy working on their own ranch.

Lucy looked troubled.

"What is it?" Momma blurted out; "is it Briella? Is she sick?"

"No, Momma, no, the baby is fine. Really, she is perfect. I can't believe what a perfect baby she is and that's the problem, Momma. I don't know what to do!" Lucy finished.

Momma had been busy unbundling baby Briella and stopped to look directly at Lucy. "Why is this a problem?" Momma asked Lucy.

Frank had excused himself to step back outside and look for Alex K. and Izrael. He made a comment that he was needing to borrow some tools and mumbled, shaking his head, as he left the women to talk.

"I'm not sure, Momma," Lucy answered as she dabbed her eyes with the cloth she held tightly in her fist.

"You look very tense, Lucy, what is it, darling and what can I do to help?" Momma said softly.

At this, Lucy opened up. Through tears and sobs she explained that she could not help comparing Briella to another baby who had been part of the family several years before. She remembered how Jane Mae had looked as a baby and how difficult of a baby she was. Lucy shared with Momma that she had had not-very-nice thoughts about Jane Mae back then, and now here she was with the most beautiful baby girl she had ever seen. Lucy went on talking about how guilty she felt for having thought those things about Jane Mae and that she did not deserve to have such a perfect child.

"Oh, Lucy, the two have nothing to do with each other," Momma consoled gently. "You and Frank have a beautiful baby and there is nothing for you to feel guilty about, do you hear me?" Momma asked Lucy.

"That's what Frank tells me every day. I keep feeling this terrible feeling of doom, like what I thought about Jane Mae is going to catch up with us and we will have to pay for my having felt like that." Lucy explained slowly. "Do you remember how we all felt about Jane Mae, Momma? Each of us had the same thoughts, didn't we Momma?

"Yes, Lucy, I do remember, and I agree with you," Momma answered. "Jane Mae was a difficult baby, and she is still a difficult child," Momma added.

"That's what scares me, Momma!" Lucy said louder this time. "Jane Mae was so difficult, and she is not a very nice child. I am afraid of what she will do to Briella when she sees how beautiful Briella is, Momma. I don't want her to ever meet Briella, or ever be in the same room with her. Does this make me a terrible person, Momma?" Lucy finished with big sigh of relief for finally having spoken all her fears to Momma.

"Oh, sweet Lucy, I do understand, and no, you are far from a terrible person!" Momma answered quickly. "These two baby girls come from very different parents and families. Our family has a completely different background than where Jane Mae comes from. That doesn't mean they are worse or better than us. We are just different. That's how God made us all."

"I get that Momma and I understand that. I just know how Jane Mae and Carolina are, and I am worried they will start trouble with our family again when they see Briella." Lucy explained.

Momma started, "I can see why you are worried, Lucy, and I have to admit similar thoughts came to me too. They are difficult people. We will be better off if we are prepared than to be surprised by what they might do. Let's think about this a little more and really put something together to protect baby Briella. She is the most important and precious soul involved."

"Thank you, Momma, thank you so much. This makes me feel so much better. I knew you would have just the right thing to say," Lucy gushed with a deep sense of relief. The two continued visiting and caring for the baby for the remainder of the afternoon.

CHAPTER 7

"IZRAEL'S PLAN"

Izrael did not know that Momma and Lucy had discussed what they had. He was still uncertain what the unsettling feeling he was experiencing had to do with. He knew it was something involving his family. Iz was very protective of his family.

Today was the first time he actually had time for himself. It was a warm Sunday afternoon, the perfect kind of day for a ride into the canyon, on Mindee. The family had enjoyed their Sunday meal, and everyone had dispersed back to their own homes. Izrael took some snacks for himself and, of course, for Mindee, just in case they got hungry. He finally was able to give himself the time he needed to think clearly.

As they rode into the depth of the canyon, Iz began to ponder some of his uneasiness. He remembered having felt it a few Sundays back while the family gathered around the table. He thought of Briella immediately and her soft coos as they ate. "That's it!" Izrael blurted out as if Mindee would answer. Her quiet snorts came out as if to say, "Yes, I get it, that's the answer, Iz!" The thought of Mindee actually answering him made Izrael grin.

Once they were near their stopping point, Iz pulled on Mindee's rein gently. They stopped in a flat area surrounded by tall pines, an area where they often stopped. Izrael loved to lay on the ground and look up to the sky if only to watch the trees sway in the breeze high above them. Many times a cloud would roll through the opening. He could lay there for hours, just looking at the clouds and the trees. He would imagine it was a production, a stage. The clouds became characters chasing each other and sometimes colliding into each other. Izrael remembered one time watching the "show" when suddenly a loud clap of thunder alerted him, he better get up and hurry home before those clouds opened up and drenched them.

Izrael laughed to himself quietly from his memory.

This outing was different. Iz had a plan to work on and he was finally beginning to understand his feelings and what this plan needed to focus on.

He began to write.

First, he wrote down his niece's name. B.R.I.E.L.L.A. What a beautiful name, he thought to himself. "Briella Suzanah" was the most precious and beautiful child Izrael had ever seen. As these thoughts of loving his niece so much pressed into his mind, he wondered why he had written her name. Suddenly he thought of Jane Mae. "What?" Izrael blurted to his surroundings. "What does SHE have to do with this?"

At that moment Izrael knew what the uneasiness was about. It truly was about Jane Mae, and even Carolina. They had yet to have seen or been around Briella. Izrael liked it that way. He wanted to keep it that way. He began to think that was the reason for his plan. However, as his thoughts unfolded, he knew one day they would meet. That was it! Izrael realized in that same moment, "How that meeting goes is what my plan is all about!" He said out loud again. He looked around at the trees and bushes, almost waiting for them to respond. He could see Mindee just beyond the boulders where he sat.

He began to add substance to his skeletal outline.

CHAPTER 8

"DREAMY DAYS"

"What are you working on, Iz, huh? What are you working on?" Josephina and Nikola almost said in unison when they found Izrael one late morning sitting under the big cherry tree in front of the house. The two giggled as they surrounded their big brother, one on each side under the tree.

"What are you two up to? No good?" Iz shot back quickly as he closed his journal.

"Are you writing down secrets, Iz?" Josephina asked in a whisper. Nikola giggled and snuggled into his side.

"No, silly, I'm working on some plans for a project on the ranch," Iz answered in a serious tone.

"What kind of project?" Josephina pushed for more information. "Is it about spies and bad guys?" she asked as she giggled and looked over to Nikola to be sure she was laughing too. Nikola had gotten distracted with some lady bugs and wandered around the back of the tree. "Hey, Nikki, come back!" Josephina blurted and jumped to chase Nikola around the tree. Their giggles could be heard from inside the house.

Momma stepped out onto the porch and called the girls in to clean up and help her with lunch preparations.

Izrael was relieved to have gotten away with not sharing anything about his plan. He opened his journal and glanced back over the pages, thinking deeply again about how to carry out the actions he had written out.

Iz leaned back against the large tree trunk and closed his eyes. Izrael dozed off, into "dreamland" as Poppa often said when he saw Izrael deep in thought. This time Iz fell into a deep sleep and began dreaming.

In the dream he was playing outside with a little girl. The girl was dressed in overalls and had curly hair pulled half to one side and the other half to the other in bouncy bundles that moved up and down every time she moved. Her laughter was drawing Izrael in as he chased her around the yard. The two laughed and played in a happy moment.

"Wait, come back!" Izrael tried all he could to yell out but somehow could not get his voice out. The little girl kept running even though Iz could no longer run. She began to get out of his sight which caused Izrael to panic and sit straight up. He woke up with a jolt and noticed he was sweating. "What was that? Who was that?" Izrael wondered out loud.

"Who was what?" Iz heard Poppa's voice and turned to find him standing a few feet away closer to the front porch. "Were you asleep, Iz? Why are you sleeping? It's almost time for lunch. Don't get lazy on me, son!" Poppa added as he turned back towards the front door.

Iz jumped to his feet and wiped the sweat from his forehead. He wanted desperately to write down his dream before he might forget it, but he knew he better hurry and follow Poppa into the house. As he rushed to the house he scratched the top of his head, from under his cowboy hat, wondering the whole time what the dream meant.

The men washed up for a quick lunch before getting back to work on the ranch.

CHAPTER 9

"JOURNAL ESCAPES"

Once the afternoon chores and tasks were completed, it was nearly time for dinner. Iz hoped to take a little time to journal again, but he was not sure how to make it happen. He headed to the barn and found a corner to sit. He quickly wrote the details of what he dreamed earlier.

The more Iz wrote, the more he wanted to know who the little girl was and why she ran away from him.

Time passed as Izrael wrote. He moved from writing down his dream to working on the plan for his family. The uneasiness grew each time he wrote. It was becoming clearer now. The plan involved Carolina and even more so, Jane Mae. This was upsetting for Izrael. He sat staring at his journal notes then suddenly slammed it shut. He felt a surge of anger, realizing that once again the two people he wanted out of his life most were still there. He heard the constant tapping again.

Izrael looked up to see the woodpecker high in the loft of the barn. He was tapping. The timing was unnerving. Izrael had chills. They covered his body and made him shiver. "Not again!" Izrael shouted to the woodpecker high in the loft. Fluttering wing sounds followed and Iz sat with his head dropped low. He began to pray.

Izrael's prayers tended to be short and to the point. This time he lingered. He sat silently at first, hoping God would start talking audibly and tell Iz what to do. After some silence he quietly moved into a time of praising God. He began to thank God for his family, for the ranch and all the provisions they were blessed with. Then Iz asked God for a big favor. He wanted Carolina and Jane Mae completely out of his life. Out of his family's life. Forever.

Izrael fell to the floor of the barn, face down and waited. He waited for God to console him. He wanted God to give him clear answers. Clear plans. He tried to be patient.

What happened next stunned Izrael. As he laid in the dirt, still face down and eyes closed, he clearly saw Carolina and Jane Mae sitting in a field. They were sitting at the fence line of the ranch property. Izrael could not hear them, but they seemed to be yelling, maybe at each other, he wasn't sure. The scene continued until suddenly he saw a flash of baby Briella's beautiful face. It was fast, but it was clear.

Izrael opened his eyes and jumped to his feet; he was sweating. Even though his eyes had been closed, he saw what the uneasiness was all about. Carolina and Jane Mae had not gone away, and he was sure they would not be leaving soon. They had not yet seen the beautiful Briella Suzanah Cleveland.

Were they yelling about Briella's beauty in his vision? He wasn't sure but he was determined to find out. Izrael felt strong that if the family did not step in and protect Briella, life would become more difficult. Izrael's plan to keep the family close would not be torn down. Not ever.

What would, or could he do next?

Izrael stood to leave the barn. He opened the doors and took in a deep breath. There was nothing like the cool, fresh breeze he met as soon as he stepped out. It seemed to clear his mind as he stood in the breeze. He could still hear the woodpecker but the sound of the breeze against tall aspen leaves distracted him, and he felt relief.

Nothing could calm Izrael like the ranch and all the surroundings. He was ready for whatever came next.

CHAPTER 10

"CHERRY PIES"

Another Sunday family meal had come around. While Suzanah and her younger daughters started preparing for the family gathering, Priscilla and Mark arrived. They were carrying freshly cooked corn from their garden. They also carried a bag full of fresh vegetables to share with the family for future meals, also from their garden.

Momma turned to greet her daughter and son-in-law with her arms open wide. "Welcome, you two! Oh, thank you for all the wonderful, fresh vegetables! Come in, come in!"

Priscilla quickly went to work getting the corn ready to share and putting away all the vegetables. Mark had walked in with a small box that he set down in the entry way and had not taken into the kitchen. Priscilla nervously looked at Mark, hoping he would read her mind about the box. Mark did. He turned to get the box and came into the kitchen.

"What's in the box?" Momma cheerfully asked. "You didn't have to bring anything else, darling. We have a lot of food to share!"

"It's, well, um, it's a ... a pie, Momma, a cherry pie. I have been practicing for some time now, but I am sure it won't be as good as yours Momma. I am sure," Priscilla answered hesitantly. "I can't seem to bake cherry pie without burning it and I am very frustrated."

Momma gave Priscilla a loving smile and went to pull the pie out of the box Mark was still holding. "She's really getting good at pie baking, Momma," Mark bumbled out, giving his wife a quick wink. Priscilla looked down blushing.

"The pie looks delicious!" Momma said gasping at the beautiful golden color of the pie, the light flakes sprinkled across the top and the weaving top crust was nearly perfect. Then Momma saw the problem. The edges were burned, and not just slightly burned. They were black. "Oh, my!" Momma said before she could stop herself.

"I knew it! You hate it, don't you Momma? I knew it!" Priscilla said quickly, holding her tears back.

Priscilla had secretly been working on her cherry pie baking for some time. She desperately wanted her pie to be as good as Momma's pies. Priscilla spent much of her life working hard for recognition from her parents. Cherry pies were her current focus. Mark often voiced concerns to Priscilla, worried she was getting too focused on the pies. Priscilla sharply told Mark it was not his concern. One day while attempting to gently discuss the pies with Priscilla, she threw the current burned pie across the room, nearly knocking over their wedding picture on a shelf nearby. Priscilla knew she should not have done that. Still, she felt determined to bake the most delicious cherry pies ever made.

During her youth, Priscilla managed to keep her hurt feelings to herself. It was in adulthood, and especially after marrying Mark that her emotions from the repressed thoughts began to surface. Mark was her safe place to let things out.

Slowly she shared the struggles of following such a perfect older sister. Often in school Priscilla found herself compared to Lucy by teachers. It gave her anxiety, as she always knew she could never be as perfect as her beautiful sister. These struggles never interfered with her love and care for Lucy. It was her own inner battle. One that leaked from time to time. This time, in the form of cherry pie.

"Oh, Cilla," Momma approached Priscilla gently and lovingly. "Of course I don't hate it. The pie is lovely! I can show you what to do to prevent the crust from burning and I am so happy to show you. Next week, when we are canning, we can work on pies too. Would you like to do that, Cilla?" Momma added.

"Oh, yes, Momma, yes, please, Momma!" Priscilla answered.

Mark was still standing in the kitchen and could not help but wonder to himself how he might talk with Suzanah alone, about the concerns he had about Priscilla and the cherry pies. For now, he was relieved Suzanah finally knew about Priscilla's obsession. Maybe the two working together would resolve the problem.

At that moment the sounds of baby giggles and chatter filled the room. Lucy, Frank, and Briella had arrived. Poppa and Izrael were outside helping carry in more prepared food.

The cherry pie issues would have to wait, for now.

CHAPTER 11

"MEAL CHATTER"

As usual for the Kammer family, the chatter around the table started out with several conversations happening at the same time. Until Poppa spoke. Everyone listened when Poppa spoke.

Poppa started, "It looks like your crops are coming up really nicely, Mark. Nice job there, son!"

Mark looked up quickly, smiled, and thanked Poppa for the compliment.

Next Poppa looked over at Frank who had just reached for a second biscuit. He, like everyone else, could not resist a second serving of Momma's homemade biscuits. "How are things on the ranch, Frank? Anything new happening?" Poppa asked before taking a large bite of roast and mashed potatoes in one forkful bite, followed by a bite of his own biscuit.

"Things are good, sir, very good. Thank you for asking, sir." Frank replied quickly. "Nothing new right now," he added to be sure he answered all of Poppa's question.

"Very good, son, very good. That's what I like to hear, that all is well with our family." Poppa piped proudly.

Izrael loved to hear how his sister's husband's work was going. It motivated him and made him happy too, like Poppa. "I love hearing all this too," Iz jumped in. "You guys are so good at what you do!"

"Thanks, Iz" Mark and Frank responded almost in unison. The girls all giggled.

More chatter continued around the table until finally getting to dessert. This time it was Priscilla's cherry pie. Priscilla had already gotten up to cut the pie and begin serving onto the dessert plates. Lucy got up to help. Soon everyone had a piece of Priscilla's cherry pie.

"Momma, your pie looks different," Nikki blurted out.

"Nikola! Where are your manners?" Momma gasped, knowing Priscilla was very nervous about having the family try her pie for the first time.

"I'm sorry, Momma. I just meant it looks different than usual. I didn't mean anything bad by it." Nikki answered quietly. "It looks delicious," Nikki added smiling.

Momma winked at Nikola to let her know she wasn't upset with her. Momma then stood while telling the family excitedly that Priscilla had baked the cherry pie for dessert and how much she was looking forward to eating a piece.

Poppa clapped proudly before filling his fork with a big bite of Priscilla's cherry pie. Everyone went silent. The only noise heard was the faint sound of Briella's breath while she slept in the small crib set up in the kitchen for her naps.

"Poppa! Tell me, what do you think, do you like it? "Priscilla asked impatiently, and nervously.

Priscilla wasn't the only one anxious to hear what Poppa would say about the pie.

He chewed slowly, looking up from his plate to see the whole family watching his every move. "What? Of course it's delicious! After all, Priscilla learned from the best!" Poppa bragged.

Priscilla wasn't sure if that was a compliment to her or to Momma. She shrugged it off. Soon the whole family was eating pie, laughing and enjoy each other's company.

When they had almost finished, Nikola exclaimed, "Hey, where's the crust?"

CHAPTER 12

"MOMMA'S GIRLS"

Suzanah had kept many thoughts to herself over the last few weeks. She was worried about her two older daughters, Lucy and Priscilla. Both had been anxious about two very different things. Suzanah wondered to herself why her girls had become anxious adults. They had been such happy and content girls growing up. Suzanah pondered over various memories which only confused her more. She decided she would talk with each of them, separately, then she prayed for each daughter, and each family member by name.

The following day began the week of canning. Suzanah was excited to have her girls over and another day with baby Briella. The younger girls were at school so she would have time to talk with Lucy and Priscilla, hopefully one on one.

After Josephina and Nikola had left for school, Suzanah double checked the pantry and thought of Carolina and Jane Mae. She had not seen or heard from them since the day Carolina had helped her clean the pantry in preparation for today. She hoped they would not intrude on her day with her girls. Suzanah immediately felt bad for her thoughts and lifted a quick prayer of forgiveness for harboring such things in her heart.

"Momma, we're here," Lucy's voice interrupted Suzanah, and she gladly stepped out of the pantry and over to hug Lucy and take Briella from her arms. Briella giggled and snuggled into Momma's shoulder as only a baby could do. "Oh, Briella, my darling, I love you so much, sweet baby!" Momma chimed.

"Momma, I just realized we will need to figure out what Briella will call you and Poppa," Lucy cheerfully said.

"Oh, goodness, that's right!" Momma almost sang back. "What do you want to call me, my precious baby girl?" Momma continued in her baby-sing-song way. Briella giggled and cooed back to Momma in the most perfect baby voice anyone had ever heard.

"Did you hear that, Lucy?" Momma excitedly turned around, "she's already talking! She is not just beautiful, Lucy, but she is very smart too!"

With that, Briella let out a loud giggle followed by what sounded to Momma and Lucy like she had sang out, "Gaahnaah" (rhymes with Su-"zanah"). The three laughed out loud together followed by gasps and an "Oh, my!" from Momma.

"What's going on in here?" came Priscilla's voice from the front door. "What is all the laughter about, Momma? Lucy?"

"Oh, you won't believe what baby Briella just said!" Lucy gushed back at Priscilla. "She said, 'Gaahnaah' to Momma, Cilla, she really did! We were just talking about what Briella will call Momma and Poppa and then she said it!" Lucy continued.

"What, really?" Priscilla popped back and rushed to wash her hands before taking Briella into her arms. "Did you say Ganah" to Momma, sweet Briella?" Briella snuggled into Priscilla's neck in her delightful way of giving love back. "Oh, sweet girl," Priscilla hugged Briella into her. "You are only 5 months old! How can you already be talking?"

Now the four of them giggled and surrounded Briella with love and attention. It was a sweet moment for the Kammer women.

Momma had almost forgotten the concerns she had about her daughters and their anxieties. As they were circled up together, she felt a peace over them, as if God was assuring her that all would be just fine.

CHAPTER 13

"INTERRUPTIONS"

The blissful moments shared by the Kammer women were suddenly interrupted by the sound of a car horn and a loud engine. Lucy turned to Momma and without saying a word, Momma knew what she was thinking.

"I'll handle this," Priscilla surprised both Lucy and Momma. She turned to hand Briella over to Lucy and hurried to the front porch.

As they expected, Carolina and Jane Mae were pulling into the drive and Carolina had her hand pressing into the horn.

"We hear you and see you, Carolina!" Priscilla yelled out. She knew they could not hear her over the sound of the horn, the engine, and Jane Mae's squeals of no doubt whining to her mother. Priscilla took a deep breath, stepped off the porch towards the long drive and waited for Carolina and Jane Mae to climb out of the car.

"What can we do for you girls?" Priscilla spoke quickly before either could say anything.

"I came to see if your momma needs any help with the canning, I know today starts your week of canning. Do you need our help?" Carolina beamed, looking over at Jane Mae who was dancing in circles and chanting a song to herself.

"No, we..." Priscilla started then was interrupted by Izrael who had been working nearby on some posts. He could not help but hear Carolina's horn and loud engine and wanted to know why she would bother his momma and sisters on their first day of canning.

"What are you two doing here? Why don't you go back to your own momma and help her with canning?" Izrael blurted before anyone knew he was there.

"Well, that was rude!" Carolina shot back.

Priscilla looked Izrael in the eyes with a pleading look to not let anything get out of hand. She knew if Poppa heard he would not like hearing Iz talking in this tone, not even to Carolina.

Izrael walked by Priscilla with a very determined look in his eyes and shot out again, "What are you two doing here?" He added, "Go back to your own home!"

"Izrael Shane Kammer!" came Poppa's voice from behind him. "You have been taught much better. Now you apologize to Carolina and Jane Mae for your rudeness."

"But Poppa!" Izrael started. He stopped after looking directly into Poppa's eyes and knew to only respond with a "Yes, Sir."

Izrael removed his hat, looked at Carolina and said, "I apologize for my rudeness, Carolina."

"Thank you, Izrael Shane" Carolina answered immediately as she started towards the front porch. By this point, Momma had stepped out to the porch and had been listening. She invited Carolina and Jane Mae inside. Priscilla stood by in shock.

Izrael and Poppa turned away to go back to work.

Jane Mae kept chanting and was now skipping into the house. Carolina followed then Momma. Priscilla stepped inside ahead of them to warn Lucy that they were coming in. Lucy had taken baby Briella to a back bedroom for her morning nap and was still with her. Priscilla let out a big sigh of relief to see they were not in the kitchen as everyone entered.

"How's all the canning coming, Mrs. Kammer?" Carolina asked loudly. "We can't wait to try all your canned goods at the county fair, or maybe even before that!"

"We were just getting started, Carolina." Suzanah answered. "We were laying everything out when we heard your horn coming up the road."

"Do you need our help?" Carolina quickly added.

"I don't think so," Suzanah answered. "We have barely gotten things going and are not very organized yet, Carolina. You and Jane Mae must have a lot to do for your momma about this time of year, don't you?" Suzanah added.

"Uh, yes, yes, we do, ma'am. We were out running errands for her. She is canning today too. We wanted to stop by for a minute and see how things are coming Mrs. Kammer, that's all" Carolina said as her eyes searched the room.

"Are you looking for something?" Priscilla asked coldly.

"Yes, for someone. Is Lucy here? I thought we might be able to see her baby. She was born a few months ago, and we still haven't met her." Carolina answered.

"Oh, I'm so sorry, Carolina. Lucy is putting her down for her morning nap. You know how much babies need their sleep. Maybe another time. Thanks for stopping by," Priscilla said to Carolina as she pressed on Carolina's elbow attempting to guide her back to the front door.

"Wait, I hear the baby, is that her crying in the back of the house? Can we see her?" Carolina said in her whiney tone she used when wanting something badly.

"Not this time, dear," Suzanah said sternly. "The baby needs her sleep and Lucy is back there with her where it is quiet. We don't want to disturb them."

At that point Jane Mae pushed by Carolina and Suzanah and started heading towards the back part of the house where Lucy and Briella were.

As Jane Mae approached the door of the bedroom, Lucy stepped out and held her finger in front of her lips to urge Jane Mae to stay quiet. "Shh, the baby is sleeping," Lucy whispered to Jane Mae. Carolina was a step behind and shot a harsh look at Lucy. "Come on, let's go back to the kitchen, girls," Lucy added calmly and the three walked back up the hallway to the kitchen.

Momma mouthed, "I'm sorry" to Lucy as they stepped into the kitchen. She then turned her attention to Carolina and Jane Mae, stepped with them towards the front door, thanked them for coming by and said a very fast goodbye.

Jane Mae could even be heard from inside the house as she squealed and whined to Carolina that she was hungry. "Get in the car!" Carolina yelled out, "and stop crying, child!"

"Thank you, Momma!" was all Lucy could muster before letting the tears fall.

CHAPTER 14

"SEEING CLEARLY"

With all the work of canning vegetables plus the unexpected drama, by the end of the day everyone was exhausted. Poppa and Izrael returned home equally as tired. Thankfully, Momma had planned ahead on Sunday to make more than enough dinner for two days. Momma and Priscilla warmed up the leftovers, Lucy tended to Briella, and Mark and Frank arrived. Everyone was hungry and ready to eat.

"I love canning week!" exclaimed Izrael as he walked into the kitchen while the aroma of so many different foods almost stopped him in his tracks. "This kitchen smells great!" he added and smiled at Momma with his big hungry grin she enjoyed seeing so much. Josephina and Nikola ran towards Izrael giggling, each taking one of his hands to sit on each side of their big brother.

"Come on, everyone, let's sit and let's eat. I know you are all starving," Momma stated lovingly as the family gathered around the table.

Poppa said a quick prayer of thanks then the ritual of passing the serving dishes began. Momma never backed off over the years from keeping table manners important. She loved the sound of her family's voices as they passed each dish and filled their plates. It was a sound she never wanted to go away. The pattern of the chatter, the sounds of the ceramic plates and bowls gently clicking against each other, the scents, all of it meant everything to Momma. She felt her eyes tear up as they glistened against the kitchen lights overhead. Poppa noticed and gave Momma that special wink and smile that still made her heart go pitter patter. She blushed and went back to listening to the family chatter.

As things settled and everyone had eaten plenty, including leftover cherry pie Priscilla shared the day before, Momma asked a question.

The family became very silent after she asked the question.

Izrael was the first to speak, "Momma, will you say that again?"

"I said, has anyone noticed a dark cloud looming over this family?" Momma repeated in as serious a tone as Momma ever had.

Suzanah had been praying for several days about the feeling of a dark cloud and finally felt a tug from God, to speak it out loud to her family. Tonight, the whole family was present. It was time. She asked a third time.

"Has anyone noticed a dark cloud looming over this family?"

What seemed like an hour of silence from the family was truly only seconds when Lucy spoke up. "I have, Momma, and thank you for listening when I came to you about it."

"You have felt it too, Lucy?" Iz asked in surprise as well as a bit of relief.

"Yes, Iz, I have and what do you mean 'too'?" Lucy answered quickly.

Izrael saw the whole family looking at him as if waiting for the most phenomenal words to come from his mouth. He suddenly felt nervous.

"What is it Iz?" Poppa asked. "Do you know something we should know?"

"No, sir, I mean I don't really know anything. It was a feeling, like Momma described, like a dark cloud of gloom, of uneasiness. I didn't understand it at first. It started a few weeks ago after one of our Sunday family dinners. I decided to focus on it in my prayers and keep notes in my journal until I could figure out what that feeling was about," Izrael explained.

"Well, did you?" Josephina asked impatiently followed by giggles from Nikola. Both girls sat back a little in their chairs when Momma gave them the look they knew meant to wait and not ask questions yet.

Izrael winked at his little sisters then went on to say more. "Like I said, I had an uncomfortable feeling, so I did just what I said. I started praying and journaling. This led me to see a plan begin to unfold; how to tackle that dark cloud. It sounds like it's time to share that plan with all of you." Izrael waited for his family to react.

Silence in the room urged Iz to continue. He shared his experience in the barn when he prayed, while he journaled, and the woodpecker's persistence. Izrael described to his family the feelings he had as well as his visions. He even talked about his dream before his time in the barn. No one spoke, no one interrupted him. It was an amazing experience for Izrael and the way he described it left the family speechless.

When he finished, Poppa was the only one to speak. "I believe we have heard everything we need to hear for one evening. Iz, son, you had an exceptional prayer experience. It is a lot to take in. We need to take tonight to each pray about what you shared with us. We can talk more after our next family dinner," Poppa finished.

"Yes, let's get things picked up and put away, girls. We have much more work to do tomorrow with the canning and preparations for the county fair. We will be together again the next few evenings for dinner. So much to think and pray about tonight," Momma added while looking at Izrael with confidence.

"Yes, Momma!" "Of course, Momma." "I'm helping!" "Let's get busy!" Each of Suzanah's daughters jumped to help their momma.

"Thank you, my darlings. We have much to be thankful for, don't we?" Momma always had the right words to say to her family.

CHAPTER 15

"WHAT'S NEXT?"

Over the next few days much work was completed in the Kammer kitchen. By the end of the week they had more than enough canned goods to share with each household, including those set aside for the fair. As they completed each day, they shared a meal and had more discussion about the dark cloud and Izrael's plan.

Things were coming together but something was missing.

By Friday evening a tension, or frustration seemed to be settling over the family. This bothered Momma more than anyone. She knew her family needed to be unified in their thoughts in order to tackle what was ahead. She was just unsure what the missing link could be.

Alex K sat next to Suzanah for dinner that evening. They were usually across each end of the table from each other. Suzanah looked at her handsome husband and asked why he sat next to her. Alex K leaned close and whispered to his bride, "I know what the dark cloud is about. I know what the missing link is, Suzanah." Alex K paused, "It's Jane Mae's father. This has hovered over us for too long. It's time to get it all behind us, my love," he finished and sat back against his chair.

"You're right, Alexander!" Suzanah said loud enough for the family to hear. This stopped all the chatter and, again, the family fell silent.

"What? What's right?" Izrael was the first to ask.

"Poppa and I were talking about the feeling that something was missing in this dark cloud looming over this family." Momma started. "We all agree and know it has something to do with Carolina and Jane Mae as well as our precious Briella, but something was still lurking out there, or someone. Well, Poppa has figured it out and I agree with him.

As the discussion continued around the table, soon all the family agreed. It was time to find out the real truth about Jane Mae's biological father.

"What do we do now? How do we find out?" Nikola asked.

"Let's just take this one step at a time, one day at a time, sweet Nikki," Poppa answered in the playful tone he often used with his youngest child.

"Okay, Poppa!" Nikki answered as she playfully threw her arms around Poppa's shoulders and gave him a kiss on his cheek. This made Poppa smile.

"Poppa, I have a question," Izrael spoke up. Everyone again turned to listen to Iz. "I remember your telling us to let that go, that it wasn't our issue to know who her father is. What changed, Poppa?"

Poppa then turned to Izrael and answered frankly, "Good question, son. This dark cloud, this gloomy feeling won't leave until we know the truth. It wasn't the right time back then. Now it is. God has led us to this point. We will follow His lead, one step at a time," Poppa finished.

With that, Izrael nodded. He trusted Poppa more than anyone. His wisdom was almost beyond Izrael's understanding.

He still had so much to learn from Poppa, and he suddenly felt overcome with peace and joy.

In his innermost soul Izrael heard these words, "It's all going to be okay."

CHAPTER 16

"SECRETS OF THE ORCHARD"

Momma's orchard was a popular place for the Kammer, Cleveland and Samson families. All three families picked their share of fruit from the orchard. Lucy and Frank loved to go into the orchard to pick from the beautiful trees and bushes. They were often seen working in the orchard, pulling weeds, and making sure all was well watered and cared for. Everyone worked hard to help keep the orchard beautiful.

Izrael was working nearby one day when he heard voices. It was Lucy and Frank. They were laughing, talking, and teasing each other. Iz could hear their giggles. They sounded so happy. It reminded him of watching his grandparents dancing among the tall weeds, falling down, hugging, and always laughing. It made Izrael feel good to see Lucy and Frank this way. He longed for that kind of love one day.

Unfortunately, not everyone in the family felt this kind of joy while working in the orchard. When Priscilla and Mark worked in the orchard it was much more serious. They did the same amount of work tending to the trees and bushes as anyone, however, they focused on growing and selecting the best fruit they could find. Priscilla still wanted the "best cherry pie ever" and the best produce in the valley. It had clearly become an obsession. Mark often reminded Priscilla to not be competitive with her own family and to give herself time to learn from her momma. Priscilla always thanked Mark and tried not to get carried away, but the temptations of competitiveness were strong in Priscilla.

On this particular day, they too were working the orchard. Priscilla and Mark could not help but hear Lucy and Frank laughing and talking their way through what sounded more like recreation than work to them. Priscilla felt a tinge of jealousy. How could Lucy call this fun? It was their livelihood. Priscilla and Mark grew a huge variety of vegetables in their enormous garden and worked the orchard with that same mindset. If either failed, their livelihood took a big hit. While they had not started a family of their own, the fields and orchard had become their family, their children.

As Priscilla and Mark worked in one area of the orchard, Lucy and Frank had started in an area fairly close by. Soon their paths met and the first words from Priscilla were, "I hope you didn't damage any vegetation during all that frolicking you two were doing!"

"Priscilla!" Mark urged strongly but with a kindness to not upset her. "What she means is..." Mark started to say.

"I know what she means," Lucy interrupted with Frank beside her, his arm affectionately around her shoulders. "This is a lifelong struggle between us, isn't it Cilla? Remember when we used to come pick fruit for Momma and you always wanted to get the best fruit so you would get more compliments and hugs from Momma than me?"

"I don't know what you are talking about!" Priscilla shot back. "Momma always gave us the same number of compliments and hugs, so we didn't have to compete."

"Have you reminded yourself of that lately, sis?" Lucy shot back quickly.

The two stepped towards each other dropping their baskets full of fruit, nearly knocking each other over. The two could be heard from outside of the orchard, bringing Izrael in to find out what the commotion was about.

"Oh, not again!" were Izrael's first words to his older sisters. "Can this squabble just come to an end finally?

Mark and Frank looked instantly at Iz and almost in unison asked how long it had been going on.

"Why don't you ask them?" Izrael answered. "They should know better than anyone. Ask them why they squabbled in here and never in front of Momma. Go ahead, ask them!" Izrael said with a big smile on his face.

Lucy patted down her skirt and wiped her hands with the towel tucked neatly into her waistline, then stated, "Come on, Izrael Shane Kammer! You know better than to start any rumors. Cilla and I did not have any differences. We just played together out here and sometimes we got a little loud.

"Yeah, right!" barked Priscilla. "You just wanted Momma and Poppa to think you were so perfect, always the one doing everything right, always the one pleasing them every single day!"

"Some things just need to stay in the past, Cilla, don't you agree?" plead Lucy to her younger sister. Priscilla did not respond but only looked down at her basket and began to pick up a few pieces that had fallen out when she dropped it.

"What? That's it?" Izrael shot out. "Why don't you tell your husbands all about those secrets from the orchard?" He continued.

"Secrets? Lucy?" Frank queried Lucy, even more so with the look he gave her. Lucy turned away quickly and began to pick up fruit she had dropped as well.

"Let's take our gatherings home, Cilla, shall we?" Mark gently reached for Priscilla to turn and walk back to their house.

"Orchard secrets can't die because no one will spill the fruit!" Izrael proclaimed as if he were the master of ceremonies and the play had just ended.

"Oh, brother," both sisters said in unison followed by anxious laughter. Everyone began picking up their belongings to go back to their own houses. The laughter did continue, but the animosity, the curiosity, and the questions lingered behind.

Lucy and Cilla had squabbles in the orchard since they were old enough to pick fruit for Momma. When they were young, they agreed to not let Momma know about the arguments. They managed to keep them a secret, a secret of the orchard. As they grew older their squabbles continued but the reason for the squabbles changed. At one time there was a boy. His name was Scott. Both Lucy and Priscilla were fond of Scott. He was a year older than Lucy and 3 years older than Priscilla. He would often stop by the orchard while the girls were picking fruit, just to visit and sometimes flirt with Lucy. He found both girls attractive, but Lucy was closer to his age. That didn't stop him from flirting with Priscilla too. The sisters fought about Scott many times, but always in the orchard. One day Scott overheard them arguing and chose not to go in to flirt with them. He just stopped going to visit altogether. From one day to the next, they no longer saw Scott in the orchard. They blamed each other. The secret, or spirit, of jealousy around Scott would remain in the orchard.

Deep in Momma's Orchard.

CHAPTER 17

"ATTENDING CHURCH"

A couple of weeks passed until the family was together to attend church on a Sunday morning. The Kammer family attended a small mountain valley church along with most other families nearby. There were only 3 churches in the valley.

The Kammer's were protestant and attended the same church altogether. When the weather was nice the family enjoyed walking to church. The shortest route from the ranch required crossing through a neighbor's land. Years ago, Grandpa K along with the neighbor's grandpa agreed that a trail should be marked to the church. Grandpa K built a gate, which helped avoid barbed wire fence mishaps to their Sunday best.

Priscilla and Mark typically walked with the family, as they were close enough. Lucy, Frank, and Briella normally drove up the road directly to the church.

The church sat nestled against the rugged mountainside. With its tall steeple, it could be seen for miles. On Sundays the teenagers from different families took turns ringing the bell, calling parishioners to church.

The pastor of the church, Reverend Melvin T. Pierce, had moved into the valley alone only a few months prior. The people of the church were not sure what to think of a single man pastoring their small church when they had been accustomed to pastors with a wife and a family. Reverend Pierce was different. He spent time going out visiting with families, trying to get to know the people of the valley. Some found him to be intrusive; others felt he was simply trying to make friends because he was lonely. A few of the ladies in the church felt sorry for Reverend Pierce being alone, and often baked him cakes and pies, bread, and even full casseroles. When he visited their homes, he would take bags full of food home with him. Reverend Pierce joked from the pulpit that his waistbands were getting tighter, and he needed to take a break from the rich desserts.

This particular Sunday morning Reverend Pierce led a beautiful service. As the people lined up to bid a good day to the pastor, the Kammer families were stepping out of the pews to join in the line. Suddenly a loud shrieking cry made everyone turn towards the sound. It was, of course, Jane Mae squealing at Carolina and Mrs. Parker.

"What are THEY doing here?" Izrael blurted in a loud whisper. This made his younger sisters giggle but when they saw Momma's look, they stopped quickly.

"Hi Izrael Shane Kammer," shot Carolina from several pews away. "What are YOU doing here? I didn't think you went to church anymore. Not since, well, you know!"

"What's this all about?" came another voice from the back of the church. The line to greet the pastor had cleared and Reverend Pierce stepped back inside to find the Kammer families along with the Parker family in an awkward conversation. "God's blessings to you all as you visit!" he added. "Don't let me interrupt although I would love to get to know all of you more. I don't see most of you too often." Reverend Pierce continued with short comments until Alex K. stepped over to shake his hand.

"Good morning, to you, Pastor," Alex K. interjected. "I enjoyed the service and your message this morning and hope you have a really nice day!"

"What's your hurry, Mr. Kammer? Do you have a big lunch to hurry home to? I don't have any plans myself actually." Reverend Pierce said in response.

"Why don't you join our family for our Sunday meal today, Pastor?" Suzanah quickly invited Reverend Pierce. "We have more than enough to share." Alex K stepped back next to Suzanah and forced a smile and nod towards the reverend.

"That is very kind and generous of you Mrs. Kammer, I accept," was Reverend Pierce's instant response.

Izrael locked eyes with Poppa and at the same time could feel Carolina staring at him from his side eye view. Izrael talked to himself in his head, "don't look at her, don't look at her, don't look at her" until she boldly stepped closer and pushed her way by him, then Poppa and lastly looked Lucy in the eyes. Carolina smiled and nodded, as she walked beside Lucy. She casually, coldly, glanced down at baby Briella who was sleeping in Lucy's arms.

"That girl gives me shivers!" Lucy whispered in a not-too-hushed tone.

Jane Mae jumped in to follow her momma, stopping to quickly glance at Briella. She began chanting under her breath followed quickly with squealing which was stopped abruptly by Mrs. Parker. She grabbed Jane Mae's hand and pulled her towards the front door of the church as they were suddenly leaving. Next, the sound of Carolina's engine let everyone know they were gone.

"Well, that was interesting!" Reverend Pierce busted out followed by giggles and laughter from the younger girls. The rest of the Kammer family began to chuckle as they made their way out of the church. Everyone but Suzanah. She kept her thoughts to herself. She felt an uneasiness that she could not quite understand. She would pray about it later, Suzanah decided.

"Come on over when you are ready, Pastor," Suzanah smiled and shook Reverend Pierce's hand.

"Thank you, kindly, ma'am. I will see you soon."

CHAPTER 18

"THE SUNDAY LUNCH"

As the families arrived back to Kammer Ranch, everyone began doing their part to get lunch together. Momma never failed to have enough prepped before church. Her goal on Sundays was to have the food ready to pull together quickly to prevent anyone, mainly Izrael, from starving.

"Momma everything looks and smells delicious!" Izrael happily said as he entered the kitchen. Momma turned and winked at her son. Lucy, Priscilla, Josephina, and Nikola were all in the kitchen helping. Nikola stopped wiping the table to give her brother a big hug. Izrael hugged her back tightly, smiling and tickled her side a little. Nikki laughed out loud and went back to the table to finish wiping it down.

Lucy stepped over to Izrael to ask about Carolina and Jane Mae. "I have no idea what was going on with them, Lucy. They seem to show up everywhere I go. I am really tired of it." Izrael answered.

"I have noticed that Iz, and I am getting tired of it too. We need to get back to the plan soon, remember?" Lucy added.

"Yes, yes, I do. It is nearly always on my mind, sis. I want to ..." Izrael stopped when he heard a voice from the porch. Reverend Pierce had arrived.

Alex K had been sitting in his chair on the porch waiting for the pastor to arrive. While he waited, he took time to write a couple of reminders in his pocket notebook. Alex K kept track of ranch business in his small notebook. He did not want to forget to pick up some supplies for the ranch. He was working on his list when he heard Reverend Pierce's vehicle pulling in.

"Welcome to Kammer Ranch, Reverend Pierce!" Alex K greeted the pastor warmly. He had been unsure, and a little anxious, about the reverend joining them. Alex K attended church with his family but not every week. On a working ranch anything can happen any day of the week. He remembered the Sunday prior he and Izrael could not find one stray from the herd. It had taken them a couple of hours and by the time they were back at the house it was time to leave for church. Suzanah and the girls were just about to leave. "Next week, darling, we will make sure to be in church with you and the girls. I promise." Alex K said kissing Suzanah gently on the cheek.

"Thank you, Mr. Kammer!" Reverend Pierce's response interrupted Alex K's thoughts. "I appreciate the invite this morning and I look forward to spending time with you and your family, sir."

"Come on in, Reverend Pierce. Lunch should be ready soon." Alex K gestured Reverend Pierce into the front room where they could sit and visit. The aroma from the kitchen distracted both men as they attempted to share small talk.

To Alex K's relief, it was only a few short minutes before Suzanah entered and invited them both into the kitchen. "Come and take a seat, gentlemen. Lunch is ready." Suzanah stated in her kind and warm way. Alex K smiled fondly and with great emotion towards Suzanah who blushed a little and led them into the kitchen.

As the serving platters began being passed, in the same melodic style the Kammer family managed for every meal, Reverend Pierce could not help but comment. "Your family is so polite and well mannered, Mr. and Mrs. Kammer. I have not seen any other family do this in such a pattern. It is almost a rhythm, like a perfect melody of a song. My hat is off to you both!"

"Thank you!" Alex K and Suzanah answered at the same time. The family all breathed out with a quiet laughter that seemed to help calm nerves around the table.

"You learn a lot about a family at their table." Reverend Pierce said gently. "Your home has a strong spiritual and warm feeling. I have a feeling there is a lot of prayer happening in this house."

"Yes, Pastor, we do pray a lot. It is how we get through things. We honor God with daily prayers," Suzanah responded to Reverend Pierce.

"It is evident, Mrs. Kammer, very evident," the pastor replied.

After some silence and small talk around the table, Suzanah let everyone know to save room for cherry pie.

"Cherry pie? Oh my, that's my favorite dessert, Mrs. Kammer," Reverend Pierce announced.

"Mine too, Pastor!" Izrael wanted Reverend Pierce to know it was his favorite. "Momma bakes the best cherry pie in the valley," Iz added. "You won't believe how good it is!"

"Izrael, you know we don't brag like that. And your sister, Priscilla, has become quite the cherry pie baker herself, don't you agree, son?" Momma answered Izrael.

"Oh, yes, Momma, I didn't mean anything bad about your pie, Cilla. It was delicious too! Momma is a great pie baker teacher!" Iz said proudly. With that and the giggles that followed, Momma and Priscilla stood to gather the dessert. Within a few minutes everyone had a piece of cherry pie and were enjoying happy chatter.

"I have to agree with you, Izrael Kammer! This is the best cherry pie I have ever tasted! I have not tried your pie, Mrs. Samson, but I volunteer to be a taste tester." Reverend Pierce added. Everyone laughed and finished up their dessert.

Before anyone had gotten up to leave the table, Reverend Pierce asked an uncomfortable question. He started, "I am curious about something, folks. This morning you all appeared to be in a difficult conversation with the Parker family. Did I imagine that or is there trouble between your families?"

At this point Alex K felt uneasy. Suzanah could see the look on his face and knew this conversation might not go well. She answered before anyone else could, "Why do you ask, Reverend Pierce?"

"When I stepped back into the sanctuary, I heard a voice asking what someone–I think she was asking you, Izrael, was doing there! That took me back a little and surprised me. Honestly, I am curious what that was about. Will you share with me?" Reverend Pierce looked directly at Izrael as he asked.

"Well, um, she, um, she used to be my friend, sort of, sir," Izrael stammered looking desperately first at Momma then to Poppa.

"Let's just say, Carolina Parker is trouble, Reverend Pierce." Alex K answered directly while laying a hand on Izrael's left shoulder.

"What did she do?" Reverend Pierce immediately asked. "Did she do something to you, Izrael?"

"Reverend Pierce, I have to be honest here. Your questions are feeling a little intrusive. We may share more with you at some point, but I prefer to not have this discussion right now. Our younger children are present. Can we have this discussion another time, Pastor?" Alex K finished. Suzanah was beaming at her husband. She felt protected and that protection was covering their family.

"Yes, of course, Mr. Kammer. My apologies. I did not mean to overstep my bounds. Just know that my door is always open to all of you," Reverend Pierce replied while being sure to look directly at each family member around the Kammer table.

"Thank you, Reverend Pierce," Suzanah said kindly. "We will be sure to remember that."

The clean-up routine began at the end of this conversation. Each of the Kammer family seemed to know what the other was thinking. The dark cloud of gloom feeling had resurfaced. It was time for another family meeting. Maybe tonight.

CHAPTER 19

"BACK TO THE PLAN"

Later in the same day, after Reverend Milton T. Pierce had left filled with food and curiosity, the family gathered around the table to talk.

Izrael started, "What did everyone think about the reverend's questions earlier?"

"He's a bit pushy if you ask me," Poppa shot out looking over at Momma while she appeared to be gathering her thoughts before she spoke. It was how Momma worked through anything on her mind. The family knew this meant Momma was praying silently, seeking God's words. It brought a silence to the room. A silence only Momma would break.

After several minutes, Momma finally spoke.

"Let's pray together" were her only words as she smiled softly at Poppa who knew it was his cue to say the prayer.

"Father, God, we seek you in all things, in all ways and with a deep love for you. As we are gathered together this afternoon around our family table, Lord, we ask that you guide our words, our thoughts, and help us to know the next step of this journey we have stepped into. We ask this in the name of your son, Jesus Christ. Amen."

Several said "Amen" softly while the sounds of deep breaths and shuffling could be heard. The room remained very quiet.

Momma said, "Amen. Thank you, darling. Now we are ready to share and make plans."

"So what's next?" Lucy asked meekly. "It seems Carolina is not going anywhere."

"I am tired of her showing up almost everywhere I go!" Izrael added quickly with a strong tone of exasperation noted by everyone.

"Yes, yes, we all agree she has become even more difficult," Momma said frankly.

"Not to mention how hard it is to be around Jane Mae," Priscilla added followed by nods all around the table.

"The Reverend didn't help either," Poppa added. "His curiosity is a bit much. I don't know if we can trust him, and it doesn't feel right not to trust a pastor!"

"I agree," Momma answered surprising the family, as Momma normally would have said something more along the lines of not saying anything negative about other people. Momma continued, "He is very intrusive and much too curious about Carolina and how our families are connected. Sounds like someone let the cat out of the bag, to the reverend. What do you all think?"

"Oh, definitely, I agree," Izrael jumped in. "I would not be a bit surprised if Carolina and Mrs. Parker filled him up with lies and all sorts of stories about me, about all the Kammer family!"

"I am sure you are right, Iz" Lucy spoke up while Priscilla nodded along with Josephina and Nikki who both understood enough to know that Carolina and her momma had not been nice to Iz and the whole family.

"Can we tell our side of the story to Reverend Pierce, Momma?" Josephina asked a bit meekly.

"Such a grown-up question, Josephina, and, YES, I believe we will ultimately need to tell our side of the story to the reverend. The TRUE side of the story, that is," Momma answered calmly. Josephina smiled and leaned in towards Nikola for reassurance and because she loved her little sister.

"I have been journaling a lot of notes for some time," Izrael began to share with his family.

Frank, who had been listening silently, interrupted to comment how impressed he was with the family, how they stick together and protect each other. "My family isn't like this," Frank stated. "We talk but you all are close, really close. I am honored to be a part of the Kammer family, and I praise God I met Lucy and can be here with you for this special time." Lucy gently touched the edge of her left eye where a tear had started as she listened to her husband's words.

"I agree completely!" Mark added. "Here, here to the Kammer family!"

This made the girls all giggle. Poppa smiled and Izrael took a deep breath as he began to share his plan with the family. Izrael felt his heart swell. He knew how special his family was and how blessed he was to have been born into the Kammer family. They would stick together through this time, and they would grow even closer.

CHAPTER 20

"HARD MEMORIES"

As the family dispersed and the two young married couples gathered their things to go home, Izrael began thinking on the past. He remembered all the difficult moments and conversations he had with Carolina. He thought of the long hard ride returning home after the first encounter of conflict with Carolina and Mrs. Parker. He remembered crying as Mindee galloped at a strong, fast steady pace through the mountain trails and roads leading them home. It made him shudder and shake his head. He also remembered how many times he had shaken his head over the past few years, in an attempt to try to remove Carolina from his life. Iz almost chuckled at the thought of shaking his head while all the memories, all the emotions flew through the air at a rapid speed. He imagined them landing far, far away, in a land he could never reach, and from where he could never be reached.

"What are you thinking, darling?" came Momma's voice, interrupting his thoughts. Iz was thankful for the interruption. His memories had become more of a nightmare than anything else.

"Oh, Momma, it's the past. It haunts me sometimes. More often than I care to admit." Izrael confessed to Momma who sat next to him on the couch in the family room.

"I know it does, son. I know." Momma answered softly as she gently patted Izrael's hand. As she turned towards Izrael for emphasis, Momma began speaking, "I know how hard it has been for you, Izrael. This has been a long hard journey that has seemed to have no end. I have watched you struggle silently. I know more about your anxiety than you realize, my darling son. I have sensed your stress level, and I am a bit worried. Nothing, or nobody, should steal your joy, Izrael. You must fight through it before any spirit of depression can harm you."

"What? Depression? Momma, do you think I am depressed?" Izrael answered in a surprised tone as he looked right into Momma's eyes.

"I don't know, Izrael. Only you know that answer. I am concerned it can happen and I am determined to help you not get to that point," Momma said firmly and lovingly. "Do you want to continue and share more with me, Iz?"

"Yes, I do, Momma," he answered and began to talk through the memories, how those memories made him feel and let his emotions lead him as he shared with Momma. As Izrael talked, he realized some of his memories were easier to talk about than others. At times he would stutter and at others he paused for several minutes, holding back tears. Momma resisted reaching out to wrap her arms around Iz. She wanted to reach out and push the bad memories out of his mind, to help resolve everything for him. It made her heart hurt just listening and watching Izrael react as he spoke about Carolina.

"Then the dream, Momma. What did it mean? I can't stop thinking about it and the little girl. She didn't look at all like

Jane Mae, not even close. I mean, she was cute!" Izrael finished in a strong determined tone.

Momma resisted a giggle that then seemed to clog her throat and not let her speak.

The two sat in silence for several minutes. Finally Momma sat straight up, turned towards Izrael, and placed her hands firmly on his shoulders. She began to pray, silently, with her eyes closed and head bowed. The moment made Izrael's eyes fill as he watched his momma, knowing how much she loved him. Iz could feel the love coming from her. He had often wondered how she could love each of her children, and Poppa, equally, with such fierce love. Momma never let any of her family wonder if she loved them. "It must be a momma thing," Iz thought to himself.

Suddenly, Momma opened her eyes. They had moistened while she prayed silently. "I prayed about your dream, Izrael Shane. God even gave me a sneak peek into it, and I understand the meaning. Let me explain, son."

Izrael gasped out loud as Momma spoke, specifically when she said she had a peek into his dream. He could scarcely understand or imagine how God could give Momma such insight, especially a visual image of what he had dreamed. He felt a little queasy as his nerves began to get the better of him.

Momma noticed. This time she did wrap her arms around her son. She held him tightly as she moved her hands from his shoulders to encircle his neck. She could feel him relax into her arms as he rested his head onto her right shoulder.

Suzanah heard Izrael sigh. She could feel his heart go from racing to a slower, steady beat. She stayed there, holding her son until she felt him fully relax. His grip around her had been tight. In that moment the memories of holding her son through the years, comforting him, and helping him get to that big sigh of relief filled Suzanah. She knew this was a special moment. The kind of moment that can only come from a momma's love. She prayed a quick, silent prayer of thanks to God as Izrael slowly leaned back into the couch.

"What is the meaning of my dream, Momma? Please tell me now." Izrael said in a hushed but forceful tone.

"Of course, son, let me explain," Momma began as Izrael listened intently to every word.

CHAPTER 21

"GETTING CLARITY"

The long talk with momma helped Izrael more than he realized. He began to notice how much better he was able to concentrate while he worked alongside Poppa. They had been measuring fence lines and noting locations along the fences where some kind of wild animal had caused damage. They knew they were going to need to repair the barbed wire while the weather was good, well before the colder fall and winter seasons arrived. Poppa had commented many times to Izrael and even with the family at dinnertime, on how much Izrael had improved over the last several months. "He's a real cowboy, this son of mine!" Poppa often blurted proudly. Izrael always strived to please Poppa, in every way possible.

As they worked this particular day, Izrael thought a lot about what Momma told him. He wanted to keep in his mind what her interpretation of his dream had meant. Some of what Momma told him made him worry but he would quickly remind himself what she said about worrying. He knew it would not help anything and that only through prayer and faith would truth be revealed, and the past could finally stop haunting him.

"Deep in thought, son?" Poppa started as the two began putting tools into packs. "You have been a little quiet today; is everything okay, Iz?"

"Yes, Poppa. I'm fine, thank you for asking," Izrael politely responded. Poppa wondered how fine his son was, but he didn't push for more. "We have done enough for a day's work, Iz, why don't you go for a ride on Mindee and clear your mind?" Poppa offered to Izrael.

"Yes, sir, Poppa! Thank you so much, Poppa! That sounds like a great idea!" was Izrael's quick answer as he worked faster to finish packing up. They had gone far into the lower part of the canyon on horseback. Poppa offered to pull the small wagon with the tools and give Mindee a lighter load for their ride.

Izrael untied Mindee then led her out of the shade she had been resting under. He jumped up onto her back, pulled lightly on her reins while saying, "Let's go for a ride girl!" Mindee neighed her happy neigh and began a light gallop out of the lower canyon, along a road that had developed over the years from horseback and wagon trails. Iz could feel the cool breeze that often developed between the canyons. Today the breeze was light and refreshing. Some days it was more of a hard wind. Izrael was thankful for the breeze and all that the mountains had to offer. They began the steep climb to lead them up and around to the other side of the property; the place they loved the most.

Izrael ran his hand along Mindee's neck, letting her know she was a good girl. He began talking to Mindee, telling her all about the dream again and how much Momma had helped him understand it. Mindee made her sounds as usual, giving Iz a feeling she was acknowledging his thoughts and words.

"Horse therapy," Izrael said to Mindee, "That's what this is, Mindee, yes, you are very good with horse therapy!" Izrael giggled to himself.

As they neared the top, Iz guided Mindee to a spot under tall pines where they often stopped. He slid down and pulled out the canteen to offer Mindee a drink from his hands then refreshed himself. Izrael reached into the side pack still attached to Mindee where he found his journal and pen. "This is the perfect time to do some journaling, girl, isn't it?" Izrael said out loud to Mindee.

He found a rock and sat himself down. He hoped he would have time to write down all that Momma and he talked about, including the ideas she gave him, to help him overcome the haunting memories.

Izrael began writing these words, "As I write these words this afternoon, I will let my mind release the memories onto the paper and leave them there, forever, for eternity. Like a death, they will rest here and not return from the dead." He remembered Momma's description of what his journaling could offer him. She suggested he write very literally on his thoughts. She thought if he wrote what he truly felt and let his emotions carry his words, there could be some healing. Izrael wanted that more than anything right now.

He kept writing. As his words moved from releasing emotions to writing down Momma's thoughts and ideas, he could honestly say he felt some relief. "Momma was right!" Iz said loudly under the trees. He was sure he heard a bird respond. This made him giggle again, to himself.

He began writing what Momma told him about baby Briella and the fears Lucy shared with her. He wrote about Priscilla and her need to make everything perfect. He wrote with love and concern for his sisters. Momma connected this to what the family had gone through with Carolina several years ago. While Iz had some trouble understanding, he kept writing, hoping that writing it down would help him understand the connections. Izrael continued writing. At one point he noticed the shade had moved. He pulled out his pocket watch and noted how long he had been writing.

He looked up and spoke to Mindee who stayed close. Always close. "We better get going, Mindee girl! Momma will wonder what happened to us. It will be time for dinner soon." Izrael continued as he jumped to his feet and closed his journal. He could feel the clarity Momma talked about. He knew he had much more to do but he was feeling a sense of understanding, and he could gather his thoughts much better than previously.

Writing. It helped. It always helped. And Momma.

Izrael ran to Mindee, jumped up, throwing his right leg over her back while calling out, "Yippee, girl, let's go for a run back home!" At that, Mindee pulled back briefly then went into full gallop. The two were almost a blur, as they zig-zagged their way through the trees then full speed racing towards the Kammer house, in the open space. The wide-open space seemed to welcome them home like never before.

Clarity. It was real.

CHAPTER 22

"PIECES OF PIE"

Eating pie has continued to be a favorite event for the Kammer family. They were well known for their cherry pies, but they also enjoyed other flavors such as peach, apricot, and apple. All the fruit came from Momma's Orchard. Poppa liked to brag how the best fruit made the best pies. Baking the pies had become a favorite activity for the Kammer women. As they baked, each step had importance. If any step was skipped, the pie would be ruined and literally difficult to swallow.

Over the next several days as Momma and her four daughters began baking pies, Momma was more quiet than usual. Her older girls began to notice and shared concern between themselves. It would be a few days before Momma began to explain her quietness. All four girls, even the younger two, knew better than to ask Momma questions when she became quiet. They knew she must be pondering something important. They were right.

"Girls, I want to talk with you about something that has been on my mind for some time. I know you have likely noticed how quiet I have been. Thank you for giving me the space to work through some important thoughts." Momma explained just enough to ease discomfort and concern from her daughters. She let them know they would have a family meeting after the next family dinner when she would talk more about all the "pieces of the pie" they would be creating.

While it seemed to be just enough to share with her daughters, both Lucy and Priscilla felt an uneasiness about what Momma said. As they gathered their things to go to their own homes, they stopped to chat with each other.

"How do you feel about what Momma said, Lucy?" Priscilla began.

"I am a little uneasy about it, Cilla, I have to confess," Lucy answered.

"Me too, Lucy. I wonder what she meant by getting all the pieces of the pie together and making sure they all fit!" Priscilla stated with a strong emphasis on the word "fit." "It's not like we can put pie back together once it is cut."

Lucy's eyes opened wide as Priscilla finished her last statement, "That's it!"

"What's it?" Priscilla answered quickly.

"The pieces of the pie! It is all about the pieces and how once the pie is cut it is not possible to go back and make it perfect again. Do you understand what I am saying, Cilla?" Lucy explained. She felt sure there would be more to Momma's thoughts, but she was also confident she understood about the pieces of the pie.

"Yes, yes, I do. At least I think I do." Priscilla answered with a tone of doubt in her voice.

"I feel sure everything will make sense Sunday afternoon, now I better hurry and get Briella home and start dinner before Frank gets back to the house. He is always so very hungry by dinnertime." Lucy gave Priscilla a quick hug and kiss on the cheek then hurried out to her car to head home.

Priscilla stayed in the driveway a minute watching her older sister back down the driveway. While she still felt some uneasiness with the pie and the pieces, she trusted Lucy. She loved her older sister and strived every day to be as wonderful of a woman as Lucy, after her momma of course. As Priscilla turned to walk back to her home, she hung her head a little. She felt shame for the ill feelings she occasionally felt towards Lucy which were truly feelings of jealousy. She knew this was sinful and prayed every day that God would forgive her and give her the strength to overcome the thoughts that came, sometimes too often.

While Priscilla walked home, she gave thanks to God for Lucy and asked that He would continue to bless her and guide her steps, as well as her own. Prayer always helped make the ill feelings go away, at least temporarily.

CHAPTER 23

"MOMMA KNOWS BEST"

It was Sunday afternoon again. The family had been to church together and were back home, preparing for their family meal.

Life in the northern mountain valley was a simple and content life for the most part. While the majority of families attended church and had big family lunches together on Sunday afternoons, it was not the same for all families in the valley.

As Momma led the meal preparations, she began to talk about some of the families who did not have what they had. Momma felt extra blessed and spent their preparation time letting all the girls know how wonderful they were, how much she loved them and how thankful they could all be for all that God had given them.

Priscilla winked at Josephina and Nikola who looked a little perplexed. They smiled at their big sister as they cornered Momma to hug her from both sides. Momma laughed out loud as she hugged her younger girls tightly, kissing them both over and over until they finally pulled away squealing.

"Go get the men, will you girls?" Momma playfully asked as she patted them each lightly on their backsides.

"Yes, Momma!" the girls answered in unison while giggling and hurrying towards the front porch where they expected they would find Poppa, Iz, Frank and Mark. The men jumped up as soon as they saw Josephina and Nikola, expectantly hungry as they were.

Poppa led the way, "Let's eat, boys. If you are as hungry as I am this won't take long." Izrael and his brothers-in-law laughed as they eagerly followed Poppa into the kitchen.

The table was set perfectly. Momma, Lucy, and Priscilla were setting the serving dishes out, the steam visible from each dish with the aroma leading the way. As was customary for Iz about food, he was the first to speak, "Everything smells delicious!"

While the family made their way to their seats, the chatter began to quiet down. Momma was still standing. Poppa stood back up to reach for Momma's seat and help slide her into place. Momma almost blushed as she smiled up at Poppa, always noticing his handsome features.

"Thank you, Alexander, you are so kind." Momma whispered as she took her seat.

Poppa sat quickly and began to say the prayer. Momma interrupted.

"Before you pray, Alex, let me say something while everyone is quiet." Momma spoke gently. "I have been doing a lot of praying and pondering on several situations in our family. I have concluded that they all have a similarity. While Poppa prays, please pray for open hearts and minds as we share and talk together this afternoon. There is much to understand and ponder."

"Yes, of course, Suzanah," Poppa responded quietly as he began to pray, "Our Father,"...

As the family routine of serving dishes passing one to the other began, Poppa was the first to speak. "We all know you have been silently praying over the past few days, darling, Suzanah. We also know God has spoken to you and we await your words of wisdom that only our Father can offer and give."

"Thank you, Alexander." Momma began. "Yes, I do have much to share."

CHAPTER 24

"UNVEILING OF WISDOM"

Momma gave her family time to eat enough of the meal to relieve their hunger before she began sharing.

"The last few months I have spent a lot of time praying for each of you. I know this is not news to anyone, as I pray for each of you by name daily." The family nearly nodded in unison as they quietly listened to Momma.

"Much has been revealed to me during this time of reflection. I have a greater understanding of individual anxieties God has shown me, living restlessly in each of you." Sounds of rustling feet and clanging utensils softly broke the silence around Momma's tender voice.

She continued, "Seeing anxiety in my children led me to pray earnestly for each of you. I have spoken individually with each of you, and you are aware that I will be sharing with the rest of the family, what I have learned and what I know."

Izrael quickly replied, "Yes, Momma" to which Lucy and Priscilla both echoed softly while nodding towards Momma."

This gave Momma reassurance to continue. "I first noticed anxiety in Izrael. I believe everyone understands why and the story behind this. I will touch on it for the sake of Frank and Mark," as she winked in their direction.

"Thank you, Ma'am," Frank responded quickly while Mark nodded politely.

"What most of you do not know is that Lucy and Priscilla have both suffered from anxiety these past few months, maybe longer." Momma began to share more. "My sweet girls have had anxious thoughts that are very different in nature, but I believe stem from the same source. These feelings of anxiety are rooted from the experiences we all endured beginning several years ago when Carolina Jane Parker first entered our lives." At this nodding began all around the table.

"The year Carolina began with her lies caused everyone much strife, as we all know. She accused Izrael of being the father of her baby, Jane Mae, and made horrible accusations of his character and status as a young gentleman. This did not settle well with the family, causing the anxiety that has surfaced in Lucy and Priscilla, not to mention every one of us." Momma stressed the latter with increased tone in her voice.

Momma continued with just enough details to keep Frank and Mark informed and up to speed. At one point Mark reacted, "I cannot believe what a vindictive person Carolina is. I have heard things but listening to what took place is a bit unbelievable, I must admit." Priscilla looped her hand into the nook of Mark's arm and squeezed tenderly while looking into his eyes with much affection.

"Yes, Mark, you are right. It was unbelievable at the time too. Carolina told many lies, and not just to Izrael and our family but to other families in the valley. She worked hard to damage his and all of our reputations. Because we are a family that sticks together and we seek after God's will and everlasting guidance, we survived it. The truth was revealed. Carolina could no longer continue accusing Izrael of being Jane Mae's father. She admitted it herself, right here on Kammer property. She indicated she did not know who the father of Jane Mae was."

After a short time of silence Momma added, "We left it at that, remember, family?" More nods. "With the proper wisdom of Poppa's leading, we chose not to search for any further truth. Until recently, that is. Poppa made the statement that it was time to know the truth."

Momma then made a statement that made everyone almost flinch, "Carolina Parker and Mrs. Parker are to blame for the anxiety that has developed in my children, and I am more than ready to do something about it. I won't let it continue. I will not!"

Poppa then spoke up. As he spoke, had anyone been watching from a distance, they would have seen the entire family physically lean into the table. They were intent in listening.

"Whatever has been revealed to you, Suzanah, we will do. I trust you more than anyone. I know you have an amazing connection with our Lord. He is in charge, and we will press on." Poppa had an expression of pride on his face. The kind of pride that is led by love, a love for his beautiful Suzanah.

Tears were seen around the table, even the men felt moisture in the corners of their eyes. Frank turned to Mark as if to say what a wonderful family they had married into. Mark seemed to understand as he smiled and quickly wiped a tear.

Momma then said, "I believe God has given us the go ahead to find out who the father of Jane Mae truly is. I believe that God knows the truth and it will literally set us free, especially, you, Izrael."

Everyone turned their attention to Izrael who had tears streaming down his face. No words. Just tears. Tears and thankfulness. Thankfulness for a family who loved him, who believed in him and who supported everything he did.

CHAPTER 25

"ENCOUNTERS AND QUESTIONS"

The next few weeks were filled with planning and preparing to connect with other people in the valley, ask a lot of questions and keep track of what they discovered.

One day while Izrael had traveled into town for supplies, he heard that very familiar horn honking down the street. He knew before he looked that it was Carolina. As soon as she came into sight, she began yelling out her window, towards Izrael. The whole town heard her as she screamed out, "Hey, Speedy Iz, is that you? Slow down, Speedy Iz! Wait for me!"

Izrael resisted the urge to run the other way, in his very speedy ability. He did not. He waited for Carolina to catch up with him. He could almost hear Momma telling him to talk with her, and not to run away.

Carolina pulled up across the road from where Izrael was waiting. He could see Jane Mae in the back seat, seeming to be distracted by something. Carolina told her to wait in the car. She then turned and began walking toward Iz. Something about how she walked and the smirk on her face made Izrael feel nauseous. He still did not run.

"Where have you been, Izrael Shane Kammer? Are you avoiding me?" Carolina shot out boldly and in a tone that shrieked a style all her own.

"I have been working and minding my own business, Carolina, why do you ask?" Izrael attempted to contain his annoyance.

"Just wondering!" Carolina answered quickly. "I have some time next week. Do you think your Momma might need help with anything?" Carolina added.

"She might need some help, yes." Izrael replied. "She and my sisters have been busy baking pies from all the canning they did a few weeks ago. I know she said they still had a lot to do."

"Wonderful! I will stop by and talk with her after I pick up a few things from the store here." Carolina answered. She started to go back to her car when she stopped, turned back to Izrael, and asked, "Why are you being nice to me, Iz? You are usually not so calm when I try to talk with you. What's going on?" Carolina asked with suspicion.

"Nothing at all, Carolina. I am simply trying to remember my manners. Momma has taught me well." Izrael hoped that was enough.

It was never enough.

"That is hogwash, Izrael Shane Kammer!" Carolina shot out. "I know something is going on and I am going to find out what you are hiding from me." Carolina jumped back into her car. As she drove off, she could be heard yelling at Jane Mae.

All Izrael could do was let out a huge sigh of relief. He had survived another encounter with Carolina. He knew if he asked any questions Carolina would not have answered him. She was suspicious enough with his being cordial towards her. He hoped Momma would be able to get more from her when they talk later.

Carolina headed straight to Kammer Ranch, hoping to find Suzanah Kammer and be able to work with her next week. Carolina wanted to find out more about what Izrael was up to, than to make money. Her momma did not work so any money Carolina made went to groceries and keeping a roof over their heads. She was tired of working. Carolina wanted a husband and she still loved Izrael. Getting close to Mrs. Kammer was her best weapon, or so she thought.

As Carolina neared Kammer Ranch she saw other vehicles. She approached slowly, easing her way into the driveway. Before she could go anywhere else, she realized MJ was standing on the porch with Mr. Kammer. "Oh, shoot," Carolina said loudly, but to herself.

Suzanah had just stepped out to give Alex K and MJ each a glass of lemonade when she saw Carolina's car. Suzanah stepped off the porch and waved Carolina in, to park next to MJ and come over to where she stood.

As Carolina's car approached, Suzanah caught a glimpse of MJ's expression. He looked upset. "What is SHE doing here?" MJ blurted out.

Alex K quickly answered he thought it had something to do with helping with pies, as he stepped off the porch, guiding MJ back towards his pick-up truck. The two could be heard talking but not enough to know what they were saying. Suzanah was thankful for this, as she was ready to ask Carolina some questions.

"Carolina, hello!" Suzanah said cheerfully as Carolina and Jane Mae hopped out of their car. Jane Mae did her usual skipping in circles and chanting to herself. Carolina looked annoyed with her daughter, but ignored her, and immediately asked Suzanah about work. "Hi Mrs. Kammer, do you have any work for me next week? I have some extra time and thought I would check."

"Yes, in fact, Carolina. The girls and I have been baking pies from all the fruit we canned a few weeks ago and could use some help getting ready for the county fair in a couple of weeks. Can you come over next Tuesday morning?" Suzanah had to think quickly, as she had not expected to see Carolina so soon after their family meeting the few days before.

"Sure, I can do that! We will be here Tuesday morning, thank you, Mrs. Kammer, see you then!" With that, Carolina turned, grabbed Jane Mae by the collar and shoved her into the back seat. "Bye, now!" was the last Suzanah heard, and they backed out of the driveway quickly.

"That was a fast visit!" MJ yelled out towards Suzanah.

"Yes, indeed, it sure was," Suzanah answered as she stepped back into the house.

Alex K and MJ visited a little longer until MJ excused himself, stating he needed to get home before his poppa sent out a search party. Alex K patted MJ on the back and bid him farewell. He then rushed into the house to talk with Suzanah.

"What was that all about, Suzanah? That girl looks as crazy as ever!" Poppa said as he entered the kitchen where he found Suzanah sitting at the table with a paper and pen, writing intently. "Did you hear me?" Alex K added.

"Oh, yes, Alexander, I did. I am sorry. I had to write myself a few notes so I would not forget. Carolina will be here to work next Tuesday, and I need things for her to do plus I made notes on what I can do to strategically get information from her," Suzanah explained.

"Great, Suzanah!" Alex K pulled up a chair by Suzanah. The two worked together for the next hour, until they heard voices coming from the front of the house.

Josephina and Nikola led the way with Izrael close behind. He stopped by the school on his way home, to pick them up. Nikki chattered nonstop during the drive home. She told her big brother all about her day at school. Josephina got a few words in but, as usual, let her little sister do most of the talking.

"Momma, Poppa, we're home!" Nikki squealed with delight, "and Bubba picked us up! We didn't have to walk. Thank you, Bubba, I love you" Nikki added with a big hug for her brother. Izrael smiled and hugged her back, leaning down to whisper he loved her too.

"This is why we are working hard on plans, Alexander, this is what it is all about!" Suzanah stated emphatically. Alex K wrapped his arm around her shoulders and gave her a quick hug and a wink.

CHAPTER 26

"THE REVEREND'S VISIT"

The next morning brought a knock on the door. It was early when Reverend Pierce came to visit. The girls had just left for school and Poppa and Izrael were close enough near the house that they heard the reverend's vehicle pull in.

"What can we do for you, Reverend Pierce?" came Poppa's voice from behind him on the porch. Momma had not heard the knock from the far end of the house, so it was good Poppa arrived when he did.

"Well, Good Morning to you, Mr. Kammer! How are you and your family doing on this fine morning?" Reverend Pierce answered after being startled by Alex K's booming voice.

"We are doing fine, thank you, Reverend. Now, what can we do for you?" Alex K sounded a little annoyed by their early morning visitor.

"I thought I heard voices," Suzanah approached the front door and opened it to invite the reverend in. "Can I offer you a cup of coffee and a biscuit Reverend Pierce?"

"I would love both, thank you, Mrs. Kammer." Reverend Pierce answered immediately. He remembered the meal at Kammer Ranch a few weeks prior. He ate two or three biscuits that day, not to mention the few Mrs. Kammer sent home with him. He looked forward to eating another, or possibly two.

"Again, Reverend Pierce, what can we do for you?" Alex K was getting impatient. He had instructed Izrael to continue working in the pens with the small animals, letting him know he would be back soon. This was taking too long. Alex K needed to get back to work.

"I am sorry, where are my manners?" Reverend Pierce responded, turning to shake hands with Alex K who took his hand and shook it vigorously. Suzanah shot Alex K a questioning look but remained calm and smiled politely at the reverend.

"Let's sit, come, have a seat." Suzanah invited the two to sit at the table.

"Again, I am sorry I didn't answer your question, Mr. Kammer. I found myself distracted with the thought of enjoying one of Mrs. Kammer's delicious biscuits," Reverend Pierce began as he reached for a fluffy biscuit from the basket Suzanah had placed in front of him. He giggled to himself.

"I have been thinking a lot about our last conversation, right here at your dining table, folks, and I wanted to offer my assistance." Reverend Pierce continued, hardly taking a breath between a bite of his biscuit, while talking. "I remember there is clearly a struggle between the Kammer family and the Parker family. I know we talked a little while I was here last time, but I want to know more and I want to be of service, to help you all through this."

Finally, as Reverend Pierce reached to sip his coffee, Alex K was able to speak. "Mrs. Kammer and I greatly appreciate your concern, Reverend Pierce. I am curious why you have taken such great interest in us and the Parker family. Can you explain that to us, sir?"

"Why, of course, I can, Mr. Kammer. Do you mind if I pray before we go any further? I should have already asked your permission to pray, and I do apologize for my delay." Reverend Pierce stated firmly.

"Please do, Reverend Pierce, yes, thank you." Suzanah answered before Alex K could say anything.

The three bowed their heads. Reverend Pierce began, "Father, God, we seek you in our conversation. I ask blessings over each of the Kammer and Parker families. Guide me, Lord, as I speak, as I share and especially as I listen. It is in Your name, Lord that we pray. Amen."

Alex K and Suzanah responded with "Amen" and thanked the reverend for the blessing.

"My pleasure, folks, my pleasure. Now where were we?" Reverend Pierce responded.

"Reverend Pierce, I asked you why you have interest in our families, and I would like to hear your explanation." Alex K stressed his words, impatience clearly coming through in his voice. Suzanah leaned in towards her husband in an effort to stress a calmness. Alex K responded with a deep sigh.

"I apologize again, Mr. Kammer. I am sure you have work to do. I will try to keep it short so you can catch up with your son, Izrael; did I get his name right?" Reverend Pierce barely paused enough to notice Suzanah nodding in response to her son's name.

"I understand he was involved with the Parker girl, Miss Carolina. Is that right?" Reverend Pierce asked rather boldly.

"What do you mean by involved, Reverend Pierce?" Alex K shot back.

"Uh, well, not really involved, but I believe there were struggles between them a few years ago, is that right?" Reverend Pierce attempted to re-word his statement.

"May I explain to the reverend?" Suzanah asked Alex K who simply nodded, looking firm and stern as he leaned back as if to give Suzanah space to speak.

"Thank you for your concern, Reverend Pierce. Our son, Izrael, was indeed a friend of Miss Carolina Parker several years ago while they were in high school. It became a difficult relationship as they neared the end of their senior year. You see, Miss Carolina suddenly stopped attending school. As her friend, Izrael visited her and her mother, Mrs. Parker, to check on them. When he arrived Mrs. Parker blurted out that Carolina was expecting a child and fully accused Izrael of being the father. However, you must understand, Reverend Pierce, that Izrael is not Miss Carolina's child's father. He tried to explain this to Mrs. Parker, but she would not listen. To this day they do not listen. Our entire family has suffered much from this accusation. In fact, I have concerns for Izrael and two of our daughters due to this situation." Suzanah finished and, again, leaned towards Alex K, this time for support from him to which he obliged as he began to speak next.

"There is your answer, Reverend Pierce. Our son did not have any relations with Miss Carolina Parker, even though she has tried very hard to convince us and others, apparently like yourself of a different story."

After a time of silence, Reverend Pierce spoke again. "Yes, folks, you are correct. I have heard a very different version of the story. Miss Carolina Parker is convinced that Izrael is the father. I hate to be the bearer of even more difficult news, but she showed me her child's birth certificate and as clear as daylight, your son's name is noted as the father."

At this Alex K stood and said in a very strong but contained manner, "I believe it is time for you to leave my home, Reverend Pierce. I respectfully ask that you take this news, keep it to yourself and leave us alone."

Suzanah stood next to her husband but added a softer tone, "Reverend Pierce, we have seen the birth certificate. I must confess that I had nearly forgotten about this unfortunate piece of information. That document is incorrect. Is there anything you can do to help us get it fixed?" Suzanah asked in an almost anxious tone.

"Well, I'm not sure, Mrs. Kammer, but let me see what I can find out. I will ask around. I assure you I will be discreet and will not tell anyone why I am asking for such information." Reverend Pierce noted.

"Thank you for that, Reverend Pierce, thank you. Now let's not take up anymore of your time today," Alex K stated, again firmly to the reverend.

Reverend Pierce shoved the last piece of his second biscuit into his mouth as he stood and sipped from his coffee. He reached to shake hands with Alex K and nodded toward Suzanah as he gathered himself enough to hurry out the door to his car and down the driveway.

"That was interesting!" Alex K exclaimed to Suzanah.

"Yes, and you handled things so well" was Suzanah's response. Alex K kissed her on the cheek and hurried out the door to find Izrael . He knew he had taken a good amount of time and was worried about how much work they needed to do.

CHAPTER 27

"MORE QUESTIONS"

"What did Reverend Pierce want, Poppa?" Izrael asked as Poppa hurried towards Izrael to help with the remaining few chores with the small animals.

"He has gotten an earful from Carolina and her mother, you know, about Jane Mae and who her father is. It was not a fun conversation, son, but your mother answered the way only your mother can and now the reverend is helping us figure out how to get your name off that birth certificate. Do you remember Carolina and her momma sending that to you?" Poppa spoke fast and forcefully.

Izrael felt unsure how to react. He felt a little numb. "Again? Why do they keep coming into our lives, Poppa? Why can't they leave us alone?"

"People like the Parkers are hard to understand, son. I don't know but I sure hope we can get some answers soon." Poppa answered.

"Yes, sir, Poppa, me too." Izrael answered but his heart continued to race. He wondered what Reverend Pierce could possibly do to fix things.

After the reverend left and Alex K had gone to work with Izrael, Suzanah sat in her chair to pray. She felt a strong restlessness and an even stronger uneasiness from the visit. She wanted to sit in the Lord's presence to listen. She and her family would need guidance. They had not expected Carolina and her mother would bring Reverend Pierce into their business. Suzanah had been working on building a relationship with Carolina, one that would help develop trust, hoping Carolina would one day open up and tell her everything. This visit may have derailed those hopes.

Suzanah continued to pray.

Her prayer was interrupted by the sound of the front door. It was Alex K and Izrael. They had come in for lunch.

Suzanah realized she spent more than two hours in prayer. She did not feel that much time had passed. She jumped to meet them in the kitchen.

"Are you two hungry?" Momma asked, looking directly at her son.

Izrael smiled at Momma and nodded. He stepped away to clean up while Poppa gave Momma a hug and a look of understanding. He seemed to know that she had been praying. He knew the look on her face after spending time in prayer. It was a beautiful, peaceful look. He could hardly put it into words, so he didn't. He just smiled.

Momma managed to get the two of them fed, enough to get them back to work within a few minutes.

It had been an interesting day. She turned back towards the kitchen to give attention to more chores when she saw Carolina sitting at the table.

CHAPTER 28

"CAROLINA OPENS UP"

"What are you doing here, Carolina?" Suzanah shot out before she could stop herself. "When did you come in? How long have you been here?" Suzanah's voice rang out with enough concern even Carolina noticed.

"I-I-I'm sorry, Mrs. Kammer. The front door was open, and I could hear sounds from the back so I thought it would be okay if I came in." Carolina answered in a hushed tone which caught Suzanah's attention. Carolina rarely spoke in soft tones. This calmed Suzanah enough to slow down and catch her words.

"It's okay, Carolina. You simply caught me off guard. I didn't hear the door." Suzanah offered. "Let me get you a cup of coffee and a biscuit," she added.

"Thank you, Mrs. Kammer." Carolina replied.

Suzanah quickly prepared two biscuits and two cups of coffee then sat across the table from Carolina.

"Thank you, Ma'am. Your biscuits are always so delicious." Carolina began. "I am sorry to show up unexpected, but something has been on my mind. I didn't know where else to go. You have always been kind to me, even when I haven't deserved it."

Suzanah sat quietly, listening as she sipped her coffee. She had many thoughts racing in her mind. She wondered if Carolina might tell her the truth about Jane Mae. Suzanah did not interrupt. She wanted Carolina to continue feeling safe opening up. She had to be patient. "Please, Lord, help me stay quiet and calm. Don't let me try to guide the conversation. Amen." Suzanah prayed in her spirit.

Carolina continued. "The new pastor, Reverend Pierce, has been coming to visit Momma, me, and Jane Mae often. We have been confused why he has so much interest in visiting with us. Do you happen to know why he is doing so, Mrs. Kammer?"

The question surprised Suzanah. "No, Carolina. I am not sure why I would know why he is visiting with your family. He has been here to visit with us too." Suzanah immediately regretted offering that information. As she expected, Carolina jumped on it.

"He's been here too?" Carolina asked with a much-heightened tone to her voice. Suzanah noticed Carolina's high pitch that was often noted, by others, as a whiney sound. "What did he say? What did he want? Can you tell me, Mrs. Kammer?"

"Slow down, Carolina, slow down. One question at a time, please." Suzanah attempted to delay answering and give herself more time to think. "He came this morning, in fact. Reverend Pierce stopped by to check on our family." She hoped this was enough.

"What was he checking on?" Carolina pressed. "He asked us a lot of questions, even about Izrael and all of you."

"What did he ask you?" Suzanah felt her opportunity to switch gears to the reverend's visit with the Parker family.

It worked. Carolina began spilling everything the reverend asked them. She talked about his questions regarding Izrael and what their relationship had been. "He came right out and asked me who Jane Mae's father is, Mrs. Kammer, can you believe that?" Carolina expressed surprise by the question. She went on, "Momma then showed him Jane Mae's birth certificate. I wasn't too happy that she did that, but she did. She showed it to him and told him that Izrael would not accept the fact and he does not take responsibility for his own child."

There it was. Suzanah's opportunity to dig further. She took a few seconds to repeat her initial prayer. She did not want her own feelings to interfere nor her protective momma side to ruin the conversation. Carolina became uneasy with the silence. She began to fidget and look around the room, as if someone had been hiding nearby, listening to their conversation.

Suzanah took advantage of the uneasiness and began with one question to Carolina. She firmly asked, "When are you going to tell the truth about Jane Mae's father, Carolina?"

The next bit of silence made Carolina even more uncomfortable. At one point she reached into her bag for a tissue. As she dabbed her eyes, she began to open up more to Suzanah.

Through tears Carolina began, "I know I need to tell the truth, to let Izrael off the hook. I am afraid, Mrs. Kammer. I am afraid to let go of the connection that piece of paper has to your family. You see, it's not just about Izrael anymore. I have grown to love this family, Ma'am. I know people think I don't know what love is. I can see why, but I do. I love the Kammer family. I wanted so much to be a part of a normal family, Mrs. Kammer. I was willing to lie and make life hard on Izrael. I so wanted him to love me, but I know I ruined that possibility. I did it all wrong."

Suzanah focused and prayed hard that her facial expression would not reveal her emotions which were all over the place. Part of her felt intense relief to hear what Carolina was telling her. Another part felt great compassion for the young woman in front of her. Yet another part, the strongest part, felt protective towards her son. She continued to be silent, hoping to give more room for Carolina to continue.

The silence worked like magic. "I'm truthfully not sure who the father is, Mrs. Kammer. That afternoon is a blur to me. I have tried to go back and think hard but every time I do I end up crying then I have nightmares again. If I don't think about it, the nightmares stop." Carolina stopped to blow her nose and take a sip of coffee and a bite of her biscuit which she had barely touched.

This time Suzanah reached across the table and laid her hand on Carolina's, as she asked her next question. "Do you think you can describe the experience to me, right now, dear?"

Carolina burst into full blown tears and sobs. She even snorted a bit. Suzanah waited patiently for her to pull herself together.

The description Carolina gave was a little more than Suzanah wanted to hear. She was mostly stunned and greatly disturbed by part of the description. Carolina had indicated many years before, when the Kammer family threw a big baby shower for her, that there had been "two of them" and she admitted Izrael was not the father. Even with this proclamation all those years ago, Carolina kept the birth certificate as a backup plan. She also admitted this to Suzanah at this time. Carolina went on, through the tears and sobs, back and forth about how much she loved Izrael, and she knew she had ruined that love, then back to what an awful experience it was with those "two" boys. Suzanah let her rant long enough to think and pray through her thoughts before speaking again.

She started, "Carolina, first of all, thank you for trusting me enough to share such intimate and difficult memories." She could see Carolina begin to relax. "Now I am wondering what I might be able to do, to help you discover who the father is."

At this statement, Carolina stiffened. The moment of beginning to relax ended suddenly. Carolina blurted out in her whiney and high-pitched tone, "Oh, please, Mrs. Kammer, can we just keep Izrael on the birth certificate, please, please?" with every "please" becoming higher pitched.

"Oh, no, Carolina. That is not possible. It is not fair to the true biological father and especially not to Jane Mae. We must discover the truth and give her a chance to have a relationship with her real father." Suzanah felt exasperated as she finished.

Carolina sat silent, crying again, this time with silent tears streaming down her face. Suzanah did feel sympathy for Carolina, but it was not enough to let her continue the lies. She felt even more determined to get to the truth.

"I see how exhausted you are after all this talk about the past, Carolina. Let's stop for today. I am happy to talk more with you. Are you still coming next Tuesday to help us prepare pies for the county fair?" Suzanah suggested to a worn-out Carolina.

Through sniffles and snorts, Carolina agreed. She nodded to Suzanah about returning on Tuesday, asking what time she should arrive and if she could bring Jane Mae. Suzanah cautioned Carolina if Jane Mae came along to bring activities for her, lest she get impatient and cause her to not be able to work. Carolina agreed. She took a few minutes to compose herself before driving home.

Suzanah also felt the need to compose herself. The afternoon had gotten away from her; she was now behind on her chores. Alex K and Izrael would be returning soon. She needed to get things done before the girls arrived from school. They would be hungry and ready for their snack. Suzanah felt numb, even a bit paralyzed by the things Carolina shared. She let herself sit in her chair on the porch, praying and mostly sitting in silence. She felt a tear, or maybe two, slide softly down her cheek.

CHAPTER 29

"TAKING A STAND"

The same evening, after dinner was eaten and the kitchen was cleaned up, Suzanah went to her comfortable chair, next to Alex K, where they sat most evenings. He was reading a piece of the weekly local newspaper. He looked up when Suzanah sat, noticing she looked very tired.

"What it is, Suzanah? You haven't seemed yourself this evening and you look pretty exhausted right now." Alex K admitted to her.

"You are right, Alex, I am exhausted. Did you see Carolina come in after you and Izrael left the house, right after lunch?" Suzanah answered. "She was sitting at the dining table just minutes after you left."

"No, I did not see her and I'm pretty sure Izrael didn't either or he would have said something." Alex K responded. "What in the world did she want?"

"She came to confess everything." Suzanah replied.

"What? Really?" Alex K could not think of anything else to say. He sat staring at Suzanah, waiting for her to say the next thing, his mouth gaping open.

Alex K's mouth remained open as Suzanah told him everything that Carolina had shared with her. He would close his mouth long enough to take a breath then slowly, it opened again. Suzanah, at one point, responded to his reaction with, "I know. It's pretty awful."

When Suzanah finished she felt almost as exasperated as she had by the time Carolina left the house earlier in the afternoon. She leaned back and closed her eyes. Alex K watched his wife. He could not help but notice her natural beauty. Suzanah did not make a fuss over make up and jewelry, as some ladies in the church. She did not need it. Her natural beauty glowed around her, causing many of the same ladies to envy her.

Suzanah opened her eyes. She looked over at Alex K, noticing he had been staring at her. She smiled and leaned forward, asking Alex K what their next step could be. The two talked well into the evening, Suzanah taking notes as they went over ideas and strategies.

At the end of the evening, they were both exhausted. Alex K ended the discussion with the following, "For now, Suzanah, let's keep this between us. I believe we have a good plan going forward but I would like you and I to take the next steps before the rest of the family is involved. I don't want to get anyone's hopes up, especially Iz."

"I completely agree, Alexander. This feels good to work together on this. We do make a good team, you know." Suzanah said with a slight blush.

"Yes, we do, my love, yes we do," Alex K answered while leaning over to kiss Suzanah.

What they did not realize that evening was a third set of ears nearby, listening. Izrael had heard their hushed voices and could not resist the temptation to sit in the hallway closest to the family room, to listen. He had done the same many times in the past. He was shocked by some of the things Momma said, about what Carolina told her. He knew he needed to do something too, but he would need to be careful. He did not want Momma and Poppa to know that he had been listening. They always told their family it was not polite to listen in on others' conversations.

Iz had some ideas of his own. The first was to talk with his friends, the three who with Izrael made up the "Four Musketeers" as most of the kids they went to school with called them. Iz was not feeling good about seeing his friends this time. He knew it was going to be difficult to talk with them. He knew they would probably get defensive. He would need to strategize (like Momma and Poppa discussed) on how to approach the subject. It would not be easy.

He rolled over, prayed, and fell into a hard, hard sleep.

CHAPTER 30

"MEN TALK"

Izrael woke the next morning feeling anxious but ready to talk with his friends. He knew it would be best to ask MJ first then the other two would join if MJ told them to. After breakfast, before Poppa hurried out the door, Iz asked both of his parents if he could make a quick ride over to see MJ to talk with him about Carolina. He wanted to be transparent, but he knew they would say "No" if they knew he had listened to their conversation the night before.

"Yes, sure, Iz, go ahead," Poppa answered first. Momma nodded and added, "I think it is a good idea to stay close to MJ, son. He may still be key to learning more about Jane Mae's biological father."

"That's what I was thinking, Momma, exactly what I was thinking." Izrael added, "You are always on the same track with me, Momma," smiling and leaning to give his momma a kiss on the cheek.

"Be careful, son, and don't be long," Poppa added.

Izrael agreed and hurried out the door then into a full sprint towards the barn where Mindee was waiting for the day to start. She made her usual happy neigh when she heard

Izrael open the barn door. "Hey girl, let's go for a ride down the road!" Izrael rang out. She always knew what that meant.

Iz rode away with Mindee. Feeling the cool breeze on his face was exhilarating. He loved these kinds of rides. Mindee did too. As they neared MJ's house Izrael felt a bit disappointed to slow down. He did not want to stop riding. When they rounded the corner into the driveway, Iz saw MJ close by the house. MJ saw his buddy coming.

"Over here, Iz, this way, Speedy Iz!" MJ called out.

Iz slid off Mindee and walked her beside him to where MJ stood waiting.

"How the heck are you, buddy? It's been forever!" MJ greeted his friend with a hug and pat to his upper back.

"I'm doing good, MJ, how are you and your family doing?" Iz answered.

After the usual pleasantries and catching up with each other, Iz began to feel queasy, unsure of how to start this conversation. He began by explaining some of the recent discoveries his momma had made in their family and the plans the family had for learning the truth behind Carolina's lies. Izrael noticed a clear change in MJ's face. He seemed to be shutting down. Iz was not sure what to do or say next.

"Why can't you put that to rest, buddy?" MJ asked Iz. "She is old news."

Izrael explained more about how it had impacted both of his older sisters, stressing the concern around baby Briella, Lucy's daughter. He wasn't sure if MJ knew about the birth certificate, so he explained that as well. "My family has endured a lot of stress and intense anxiety since Carolina and her momma moved into the valley, MJ. We are at our wits end needing to get some closure on everything. Can you understand that?" Iz paused to give MJ time to reply.

"I can sure understand that Iz, it makes a lot of sense," MJ finally replied. "I can tell you what I know, buddy, but it is not much."

The two spoke for over an hour. The more MJ talked; the more questions Izrael had. It was as if MJ was talking in circles. This made Izrael's head spin. He became more confused and began to doubt whether MJ was telling the truth, or at least all of the truth. This made him sad. Finally, Izrael took a deep breath and said in a strong and forceful tone, "Dang it, MJ, tell me everything! I know you have some secrets you aren't telling me. I am tired of playing games. This is ridiculous. I thought you were my best friend! Best friends don't lie to each other. They listen to each other; they confide in each other and most of all they TRUST each other!"

MJ felt his eyes filling with tears. He worked hard to hold them back until finally they burst forth, opening like a damn holding tons and tons of water with no strength left in it to hold it any longer. At that moment, MJ was scared. He wasn't sure how his buddy would react. The tension was intense, and evident.

CHAPTER 31

"DISBELIEF"

During the ride home after leaving MJ, Izrael felt many different emotions. The strongest was sadness. The hurt in knowing MJ had kept what he knew a secret from him, his "best friend!" The sadness was turning into anger. He would talk with Momma and Poppa, even the whole family about what MJ told him. He wasn't sure it would be fit for his younger sisters to hear so he would consult Momma first, to ask her opinion on that.

When he arrived home, Izrael freshened Mindee's water trough and filled a bucket with her favorite feed. He heard Poppa step into the barn. "How did everything go with MJ, Izrael?"

"Oh, Poppa! I don't even know what to think or say. He said he gave me all the truth this time, but it is ugly. Really ugly, Poppa." Iz felt his anxiety getting the better of him. At the same time he felt nauseous and could feel the sweat building under his sleeves and down his back.

"Okay, son, take a deep breath. Give yourself a few minutes, then let's talk," Poppa replied as he stepped back out of the barn and out to the corral where he had been working on some of the posts.

Izrael felt a calm and peace beginning to come over him. He thought earlier he wanted to talk with Momma but repeating some of the things MJ said, to his momma, did not seem right. Maybe telling Poppa was a much better idea. Iz took his time. As he brushed Mindee's coat, he reflected on what MJ told him. "Ugly, that's all it is, just ugly!" he murmured to himself. Mindee snorted back softly. Izrael took a deep breath then stepped out of the barn and walked over to Poppa.

Poppa was hammering on a post and did not hear Iz approach. "I'm ready to tell you about my visit with MJ, Poppa" was all Iz needed to say. The two sat on a couple of make-shift benches. MJ had been more descriptive than Izrael felt comfortable repeating, even to Poppa, so he rushed through some of the details. As Izrael spoke, he stopped often to shake his head. At one point he leaned over with his elbows on his knees, hands to his forehead and gasped for air.

"It's okay, son. Take your time." Poppa encouraged.

"It's just so ugly, Poppa. I can't believe I ever considered them my friends. Even MJ! I always trusted him. I relied on him, and I even confided in him so many times. I remember telling him things that Carolina said to me." Izrael went on for several minutes talking vividly about his friendship with MJ. When he stated his other friends' names, Benji and Cliff, Izrael's voice tone changed. It became deeper, more deliberate and filled with anger.

"Woah, woah, there son. Take it easy. Keep talking, this is all in the past." Poppa tried to bring calm and reality into the moment.

Izrael was struggling with slowing down enough to calm himself down. He felt so much anger. The three friends he grew up with betrayed him in the worst way possible. At this point he ran out of words.

CHAPTER 32

"THE REAL STORY"

Later the same day, Alex K found time to fill Suzanah in on what MJ had confessed to Izrael. The shock was enough to cause Suzanah to spend some quiet time in prayer. She replayed, in her mind, some of the things Carolina had told her, compared to what Alex K said. Something did not quite match up. She would need to ask Carolina a couple more questions to try to put more of the pie pieces together.

At first Izrael felt uncomfortable when Poppa asked him to sit and talk. He and Momma were already seated at the kitchen table. Izrael could not stop thinking about what MJ had described. The visual image was draining him mentally.

As he sat, he noticed Momma had pulled out some freshly cut slices of cherry pie. "Wow, Momma, we never eat cherry pie in the middle of the afternoon! What's the occasion?" Iz burst out before thinking.

"No occasion, son, just a special treat. I think we all need a little comfort food." Momma stated emphatically.

As they each began piercing their own piece of pie, Izrael's mind began to slow down. He felt the calm in the room and reminded himself of the safety in talking openly with both of his parents.

He began, "Momma, some of what MJ told me is really ugly. I truthfully cannot get as graphic as he did. I won't talk that way in front of you, Momma."

"I understand, Iz. Just share what and how you can. Poppa told me a lot of what you told him earlier," Momma answered softly.

"Well, MJ described it being a warm afternoon one day after school. He, Benji and Cliff had just left in MJ's pickup truck when they saw Carolina walking home. Benji told MJ he would give him a dollar bill if he gave her a ride home. MJ said he agreed and pulled over to offer her a ride. Carolina said no and kept walking. MJ stopped the truck and Cliff jumped out, hurried his step, and caught up with Carolina. The two were talking and walking fast. MJ and Benji were still in the pickup. In fact, MJ said he was still driving very slowly behind Cliff and Carolina at that point. All of a sudden Cliff was pushing Carolina's arm and coaxing her towards the thick brush alongside the road. Carolina started screaming at Cliff. All MJ understood in her screaming was 'No, and, let go!' but Cliff kept pushing her. MJ stopped the pickup and Benji jumped out. By the time MJ got around the truck Benji had helped Cliff get Carolina out of sight. The three were behind some tall, thick bushes."

Izrael stopped to take a long drink of water from the glass in front of him. His hand was shaking as he set it back down. Momma reached over to touch the top of his hand gently, letting him know it was okay to keep talking.

"MJ told me he felt like his feet were stuck to the ground, like they were glued down so he couldn't move. He could hear muffled screaming. Finally he gained his composure and took off towards the bushes where the three had disappeared. When he found them, Carolina was on the ground crying, trying to cover herself up. Cliff had a wild look in his eyes and Benji was grinning a horrible grin. MJ was sure of what had just happened. He looked at Cliff and Benji and yelled as loud as he could yell, "WHAT DID YOU IDIOTS DO? WHAT'S WRONG WITH YOU BOTH?"

At this point Momma cringed and stood to start the kettle on the stove. "I'm sorry, Momma. I know that was awful, are you okay?" Izrael asked.

"I'm okay, Iz, just give me a minute." Momma continued the process of making tea. It appeared she was moving through the steps but not realizing what she was doing. Poppa got up and helped Momma finish the tea and fill three cups full.

They returned to the table with the steaming cups of tea. Izrael was thankful for the few minutes to pull his thoughts back together.

He continued, "This is when MJ described Cliff and Benji running away. He said they ran out of the bushes and down the road before he could even think what to do next. He realized at that point that Carolina was still on the ground crying. He dropped to his knees and asked her if she was okay, knowing full well that she wasn't okay. Carolina cried and sobbed for what MJ said seemed to be hours. It was only minutes. Finally she stood, straightened herself up and appeared to pull herself together very well. Again, MJ asked if she was okay. The next part is pretty unbelievable in my opinion," Izrael noted clearly.

"This is what MJ said next, Momma, Poppa. I was shocked." Izrael then quoted MJ, "Carolina looked me straight in the eyes and told me to forget what had just happened, like it never happened, and she warned me not to tell you, Iz, or she would tell everyone in the valley that I did that awful thing to her. Iz, buddy, I promise you that is exactly what happened!"

Izrael explained to Momma and Poppa how he had questioned MJ on why he would make her that promise and especially why he kept it all these years. Izrael pushed MJ on how he could keep those kinds of secrets from someone he called his best friend.

Izrael leaned back in his chair, tears on the edge of his eyelids daring to trickle down his cheeks. He took a deep breath and closed his eyes. The tears fell openly, as if the dam had broken and they were free to run loose.

Momma and Poppa sat in silence. Momma's eyes were filled with tears while Poppa's looked enraged with anger. Neither said another word.

CHAPTER 33

"TUESDAY'S COMING"

The next couple of days left Izrael, Alex K and especially Suzanah feeling a little numb. The truth of what happened to Carolina had finally come out and none of the three felt ready to do anything with it. Suzanah went through the motions of her day, realizing the following day was Tuesday. Carolina would be at her door wanting to earn money by helping with the pie baking. "Pies!" Momma blurted out to the empty room. Suddenly reality snuck back into Suzanah's mind, reminding her that her daughters and granddaughter would be there too. She needed to warn them but was she ready to tell the horrid story to her daughters? She knew she had no other option.

Suzanah walked over to visit with Priscilla who Suzanah found in the garden pulling weeds. When Priscilla saw Momma walking over, she stood shaking off the dirt and wiping her hands quickly. The two went into the house where Priscilla offered Momma a cup of tea. The shock on Priscilla's face left Momma again feeling exasperated. She knew Priscilla was a strong woman, but she worried about anxiety creeping back into her daughter and overwhelming her. They talked through some of that before Momma headed back home. The two had decided to tell Lucy after she arrived the next morning, hoping she would arrive before Carolina. Their backup plan would be for Priscilla to take Lucy aside and tell her the horrible story.

CHAPTER 34

"ONCE A LIAR ALWAYS A LIAR"

The next morning came quickly. Priscilla arrived extra early to be sure to catch Lucy. She hoped she could talk with her outside before they had time to get busy on the pies.

Thankfully, Lucy arrived early too. Priscilla met her at the car and began helping Lucy gather up Briella and everything she had packed up for the day of baking.

"What's going on, Cilla?" Lucy immediately questioned her sister. "You seem anxious, tell me what happened, please!"

Priscilla didn't hesitate. She immediately told Lucy everything Momma had told her. Lucy was stunned. She stopped in her tracks, holding the bags she had filled earlier that same morning, almost dropping an item from the bag. Priscilla continued talking, assuring Lucy that Momma, Poppa, and Izrael had a plan and all she and Lucy needed to do for now was to go along with whatever happened next. All Lucy could do was to nod in agreement. It was enough, for now.

Momma reached for Briella as her daughters entered the kitchen. She kissed Lucy on the cheek, noting the moistness in the corner of her eyes. Momma gave Lucy a reassuring nod, hoping Lucy would feel confident that everything would work out. Lucy nodded back, understanding Momma's gesture. She took a big breath, setting down the bag she was still holding and going into action alongside Priscilla.

Momma was still holding baby Briella when the door opened again. All three Kammer women stopped and stared at the doorway as Carolina and Jane Mae entered.

"What's wrong with everyone? You all look like you just saw a ghost!" Carolina shot out while pushing Jane Mae through the doorway.

"Good morning, Carolina. We were just getting started. You can set your things down over here." Momma quickly went into action guiding everyone into pie baking mode. She stopped briefly to hand Briella over to Lucy who stepped out of the kitchen and down the hall where Briella took her naps while at Ganah's house. Lucy realized at that moment they still didn't know what Briella would call Poppa. She wondered out loud what made her think of that at a time like this!

Meanwhile, in the kitchen things were falling into place. Carolina noticed Lucy slipping out of the room with Briella and asked boldly, "Why don't you want me to see that baby? Why can't we spend time with her?"

"Oh, no that's not what happened. Lucy has the baby on a strict schedule for her naps and this is the time of day she takes her morning naps." Momma answered, "she will be up and out here with us after she wakes up."

"I see," was all Carolina muttered almost under her breath.

Soon the ladies were all busy preparing to bake pies. So many steps were involved in prepping that they each took a job. It looked like an official assembly line. The timing was critical as the step before each was completed. The room became quiet with the only sounds coming from the patting of the dough followed by rolling the dough, then jars opening, spoons clinking against the glass, canned fruit hitting the pan filled with dough and finally the last step. Priscilla had volunteered to weave the dough at the top. She had grown to love this step. It was therapeutic for her these days.

Carolina found herself right in the middle of all the Kammer women, being the one to spoon the fruit into the pans. She was feeling uneasy. Everyone looked up then towards Lucy when Briella awoke from her nap. Her cry was so sweet sounding, Carolina thought to herself. She stated loudly, "That baby don't scream like a regular baby! Jane Mae was born screaming that awful scream she still screams after all these years!" Carolina added.

Momma was relieved to realize that Lucy had left the room before Carolina made her statement. She turned towards Carolina, "Why don't we fill our cups and go sit on the porch while Priscilla kneads the next batch of dough, Carolina. It's a pretty day out there."

"Uh, okay, why?" was all Carolina said as Suzanah coaxed her towards the front door and the porch.

"I was hoping we could have a minute alone," Suzanah began. "Last week when you were here you shared a few things with me, dear. I wanted to check in with you and ask if there was anything else you would like to talk about."

"Oh, that!" Carolina stammered. "I was just feeling a bit, um, kind of emotional that day, Mrs. Kammer. You know how us girls can get sometimes."

At that moment, Jane Mae appeared on the porch, immediately whimpering to Carolina about seeing a bee and how it almost stung her.

Suzanah looked over at Jane Mae and felt compassion. She turned to Carolina and asked, "I know you and your momma teach Jane Mae at home, but have you ever thought about putting her in school?"

"No, no, we don't need her in school. She learns everything she needs to know about life from my momma and me, Mrs. Kammer, truly, she's doing great!" Carolina sounded as if she were trying to convince herself more than anyone.

Suzanah didn't push. She wanted Carolina to talk about Jane Mae's biological father. She knew the likelihood was not very promising this morning. Maybe later. She would be patient and wait.

When the two entered back into the house, Lucy was nursing baby Briella in the sitting room. Carolina resisted walking towards them and rather followed Suzanah into the kitchen.

The rest of the afternoon was spent with the same rhythmic routine in the assembly line of pie baking. Suzanah could not keep her mind from racing back and forth from what Izrael had discovered to the things Carolina told her last week. She wanted desperately to connect it all and help put the pieces of the pie together, box it up and place it on the shelf called, "The Past."

Carolina did not seem as willing to be open today as she had been the other day, until Lucy and Briella stepped into the kitchen.

Carolina turned and looked at Briella. She could not help herself but comment on how beautiful Briella was. She bluntly said, "That baby is beautiful! Why is she so beautiful when mine was born so, so, so, well not beautiful like that baby!"

"Maybe because your baby is not a real Kammer!" Priscilla could not help herself. The words tumbled out like a flowing river after the winter snows had melted.

Momma gasped. Lucy froze. Everyone's eyes were on Carolina.

"What did you say?" Carolina shot out forcefully and in a tone that meant she was ready for a fight.

"There's no way your baby is a Kammer baby!" Priscilla shot out again. "You said it yourself! Kammer babies are beautiful and Jane Mae, well, let's be honest. She isn't beautiful!"

Priscilla looked down as soon as she saw the look on Momma's face. Lucy too. They were shocked.

Momma finally stepped forward and in between her girls and Carolina. "There's no need to say these things or get any more upset than we already are, girls. Come, Carolina, let's go back out to the porch." Suzanah attempted to guide Carolina back outside.

"NO!!" Carolina screamed this time. "I will NOT listen to anything any of you have to say! Jane Mae's daddy is Izrael Shane Kammer, and I have the birth certificate to prove it! You Kammer's just leave us alone!" With that, Carolina grabbed her belongings, raced to the front door, all the while yelling out to Jane Mae to hurry herself up and get into that car or else!

Once the shock of what just happened began to settle, an eerie silence took over in the room. No one breathed. Even Briella seemed to know not to make a sound.

Finally, Momma spoke up, "I have truly experienced first-hand; once a liar, always a liar."

CHAPTER 35

"LET'S TAKE A BREAK"

Over the next few days, everyone in the family felt the need to take a break from the drama.

Lucy noted that even Briella had been a little fussy for a couple of days but was back to her normal happy self.

Izrael felt the stress and anxiety more than anyone, so he thought, although Momma seemed to experience the same.

"So much has happened over the last few weeks, Iz. It's good for us to walk away from it and just do our normal life." Momma's words rang like a melody for Izrael. He knew not to ask how she was thinking the same as he had been thinking because it happened so often. It was just the way they connected.

"I agree, Momma. I think everyone needs some time to get back to normal and let things kind of settle." Izrael added to Momma's words.

"Yes, and we know there is always so much to do around here. What, between the house and the barn, not to mention the animals and all the work you and Poppa do every day. Well, this ranch is not going to take care of itself, now is it, son?" Momma said with a little extra tone in her voice to add a sense of playfulness.

Izrael knew Momma was not feeling playful about everything that had taken place the previous few weeks. He knew she needed time to let things settle into her heart and mind before taking any steps forward. Izrael knew Momma would spend time praying about everything and for everyone involved. This was a great comfort to Izrael. His faith in God was due in great part to Momma's faith. The way she turned to God for everything was one of Momma's greatest strengths. He remembered seeing her drop to her knees in front of the family when Grandpa K had gotten sick. Her prayers helped he and Poppa make it over the mountain to see Grandpa and Grandma K that cold winter several years ago.

Momma interrupted his thoughts, "Let's get everyone together again Sunday, Iz. We will have a few days to think and pray, then back to our plans."

"Sounds good, Momma, sounds very good," Iz answered quickly.

CHAPTER 36

"CHURCH GOSSIP"

Sunday morning came quickly. The family met together outside of the church before walking in and sitting as much together as possible. Most Sundays they would sit among 2 or 3 pews but this week the church was full. They sat in family groups. Priscilla and Mark were the last to find two seats together. As soon as they sat, the couple behind them began whispering quite loudly.

"She's one of them!"

Priscilla turned quickly and immediately recognized Mrs. Whittaker. Priscilla had gone to school with the Whittaker's daughter who had moved to a city not too far away.

"Good morning, Mrs. Whittaker, how are you? Did you say something to me?" Priscilla managed to keep her sarcasm to a minimum.

"Oh, Priscilla, darling, I didn't recognize you," Mrs. Whittaker covered up her comment. "How are you dear? And how is your delightful mother? I haven't spoken with Suzanah in quite some time."

"For good reason!" Priscilla mumbled under her breath followed by a quick, "She is doing very well, thank you for asking. She and Poppa are right behind you, in fact."

Mrs. Whittaker turned to smile and nod at Suzanah then leaned forward, picked up a pew Bible and began flipping through the pages.

"She needs to stop flipping pages and read something in that Bible!" Priscilla whispered to Mark, who didn't answer. He reached his arm around Priscilla to show his support and love.

Suddenly the booming voice of the Reverend Milton T. Pierce got everyone's attention.

"Good morning, church!" Reverend Pierce began. I would like us to all stand and sing together.

The service ended on a nice note with pleasantries all around. Priscilla could not wait to get to Momma and the family to share what Mrs. Whittaker had said when she and Mark sat in front of her.

It was too late. Mrs. Whittaker was already hugging Momma and shaking hands with Poppa. It would have to wait.

The rest of the time at church passed with no further drama. Soon the family was together at Kammer Ranch. The meal came together quickly. Momma's roasted chicken with potatoes was exactly what everyone needed after a hard week, not to mentions the whispers everyone seemed to hear at church.

Priscilla sat up straight, "Do you mean to tell me that I was not the only one," then correcting herself, "WE were not the only ones to hear whispering about our family?" Priscilla's hand was still waving back in forth in front of Mark, until he took it and gently set it to her side on the table. This made Priscilla chuckle to herself as she looked into Mark's gentle eyes.

"Oh, there was plenty of whispering going on inside that church and it wasn't praying!" Izrael shot out.

Nikola sat on one side of Izrael while Josephina at the other side, as usual. "What were they whispering about?" Nikola asked innocently. "Are there church secrets we don't know about?" She giggled a little while smiling and looking around at everyone.

Josephina reached behind Izrael to softly tap Nikola on her shoulder. Nikki quickly reached up to hold her sister's hand.

"I'm sorry, Poppa and Momma!" Nikki added quickly.

"It's okay, my darling. Do not worry yourself about this. There were many comments heard at church and most of it was not very nice." Momma said in her matter-of-fact way. "We will talk about this more later," she added.

As everyone helped clear food and plates from the table, Poppa suggested they all meet in the family room where they could sit more comfortably.

"There seems to be a lot of gossip going around the community about the Kammer family," Poppa started. "I am not sure how that started but we might all be able to guess who started it."

"I have no doubt it is Carolina, Poppa, " Izrael spoke next. "Why can't she just leave us alone?" he added in an exasperated tone.

"She wants you to marry her, Izrael. That part is obvious." Priscilla stated bluntly. "My guess is she is telling everyone that your name is on Jane Mae's birth certificate, and you won't marry her and take care of them. I think she is nervous that the truth may come out soon. She wants to make everyone believe her lies and feel sorry for her."

"I agree with Cilla," Lucy stated next. "I can't imagine what else everyone would have been whispering and gossiping about us in church!" Frank nodded in agreement with his wife.

"We are so close to the truth, we must keep working on this until we know who the father is and have that birth certificate corrected," Momma said. "I think I know who can help us do that."

"Reverend Pierce!" Poppa said quickly as he patted Momma's hand.

"Yes, that's right, Reverend Pierce said he would do what he could to help us clear things up and get the right name on Jane Mae's birth certificate. I think it is time for him to help us." Momma finished up.

As the conversation slowed down, Lucy and Frank gathered up Briella to head home. The rest of the family followed. Soon it was only Izrael, Momma and Poppa sitting in the family room.

"Do you really think he can help us, Momma?" Iz asked with a pleading in his eyes.

"I'm not sure, Izrael, but it is definitely worth a try!" Momma answered. Poppa agreed.

"The three of us will go pay a visit to the Reverend Milton T. Pierce tomorrow morning," Poppa announced, "and I hope he knows better than to try to get out of helping us."

CHAPTER 37

"A CRITICAL VISIT"

The walk to the church was quiet. Poppa, Momma, and Izrael knew that the outcome of their visit with Reverend Pierce was critical to Izrael's future. This made Izrael's stomach cramp up. He never liked being the center of attention, especially when it had to do with Carolina Parker. His name was documented as the father of a little girl. It seemed for the first time he felt sadness for Jane Mae. She was innocent in all of this crazy drama her mother had created.

"Why? Why did she have to put me in the middle of all her lies?" Izrael didn't realize he said this out loud until he felt Momma's touch to his right arm. No words were needed. He knew both Momma and Poppa felt the same way. They had discussed it so many times he wondered what they might have talked about through the years had it not been for Carolina. Iz then physically shook his head, as he had done so many times before. The only result from this gesture was it helped him think of something else.

Reverend Pierce was outside as the three Kammer family members arrived at the front of the church. It was as if he knew they were coming and was waiting for them. This gave Izrael shivers.

"Good day, folks, good day! Welcome! Come, let's go inside. The wind is a bit chilly this morning, Reverend Milton T. Pierce said as he urged them indoors.

"Thank you, Reverend Pierce," Alex K responded first and offered his hand towards the reverend. Suzanah smiled and looked down quickly, not offering her hand. Izrael stepped forward to shake Reverend Pierce's hand, but he had turned his back to open the front door of the church. As he stepped into the church, he felt the reverend's hand on his upper back while he greeted Izrael. Izrael turned to nod while removing his hat. Alex K too removed his hat.

As Iz looked around the empty sanctuary, he realized he had never been inside the church other than on Sunday mornings for worship. It felt different. It held an empty, almost haunting feeling that made Iz shudder a little. His eyes met Momma's as they turned to follow Reverend Pierce to the office area. He led them down a long hallway into a corner office. They walked by the church secretary who hardly looked up as they passed by.

Reverend Pierce had a small but tidy office. There were bookshelves on every wall, filled with many books, so many Izrael wondered if it was possible for one man to read so many. His answer came almost immediately, as Reverend Pierce had been watching Izrael.

"Yes, young man, I have read every single one of those books," he said proudly. "Most of them were gifts although I purchased a few myself. My own momma and poppa started me off with my first Bible as well as the set of reference books you see at the top of that shelf there, Izrael," Reverend

Pierce said while pointing to the top of the furthest shelf from the entryway.

"Please, everyone, come in. Have a seat. Let me grab another chair from the secretary's office. I'll be right back," Reverend Pierce said quickly as he stepped out of the office.

This gave Izrael a minute to take a deep breath while making eye contact with both Momma and Poppa. Momma looked calm and collected but Poppa seemed a bit nervous, Iz thought to himself.

"Here you go, young man, you can have this chair," the reverend said to Izrael while giving him a folding chair that looked like it had seen much better days. Izrael took the chair graciously.

"How can I help you folks?" Reverend Pierce started. "I know there has been a lot of talk around the community recently. Yesterday seemed a bit restless in the church. I could sense some anxiety and felt pretty certain there was some gossipy chatter around the pews. I may need to preach about gossip next week, in fact!"

"Yes, sir, that is why we are here, Reverend Pierce," Alex K replied while looking at Suzanah.

Suzanah sat up straight, smoothing the top of her skirt across her lap. "Yes, Reverend Pierce, my husband is correct. We are here about the gossip that seemed to be focused on our son, Izrael Shane Kammer. We are seeking your help to stop the gossip and again to ask your help with another issue."

"Of course, yes, I am here to help you, Mrs. Kammer. What can I do?" Reverend Pierce asked quickly.

"Do you remember our conversation the day you stopped by unexpectedly?" Momma asked.

Feeling a little embarrassed, Reverend Pierce answered, "Yes, yes, I do, ma'am. I certainly do. You asked if I knew of any way to get Jane Mae's birth certificate corrected. I assume that is what you are asking me, Mrs. Kammer?"

"You are correct," Alex K said firmly and in a tone that made the reverend sit up taller.

"I, I, I, well, I have asked around a bit, but I have not discovered what can be done about the birth certificate, being a legal document and all." Reverend Pierce sounded nervous.

"I am not that little girl's father!" Suddenly Izrael was on his feet again. He felt anxious and worried that there was nothing anyone could do to fix this problem. Suzanah quickly turned to Izrael, whispering something as Iz sat back down in his chair.

"I understand, son, I do. These matters are difficult," Reverend Pierce continued. "I have asked enough people to know that you will need to hire an attorney. Now, do you know who the real father is, have you asked Carolina that question?"

Suzanah felt Iz begin to stand again. She reached over to lean her arm on top of Izrael's arm and began to speak emphatically. "We have asked that question, not once but many times. Very recently I had an opportunity to speak with Carolina and she shared some interesting news with me, Reverend Pierce. Carolina Parker was raped by possibly two boys. Of course, we do not know which of the two boys is Jane Mae's biological father, Reverend Pierce." As Suzanah leaned back she felt Izrael's arm under hers begin to relax. She squeezed his arm lightly as she added, "and my son is not one of them."

"I see" was Reverend Pierce's initial response. After a long pause of silence, he began, "Carolina did not share this with me and I can understand why a young lady would not say so much to a male, let alone a pastor. It does bring up a lot more concern about her stability and why she would choose to make up a lie. I can understand your frustrations as a family much more now," he added as he looked at each one in the eyes.

"Thank you, Reverend Pierce," that is a relief to hear you say this, Alex K replied. "We have been in much turmoil since the day Carolina told Izrael she was pregnant. This has literally changed the course of our lives. We have not known what to do so we have offered our help when they need it. I believe some of that has translated to acceptance of the child as a Kammer child and that she is not." Alex K heard himself state the last statement rather loudly. He quickly apologized for his tone.

"It's okay," Reverend Pierce answered with his hand up in the air. "I get it. I would feel the same way if I were in your shoes, Mr. Kammer."

"I happen to be friends with a pastor in the big city," Reverend Pierce stated, meaning the town where families did their shopping close by. This made Izrael chuckle. He felt some relief hearing a lighter tone to the conversation. "I can talk with him tomorrow. I have a few errands to run for the church so I will stop in to see him. I believe his brother is an attorney but I'm not sure what kind of work he does. Will it be okay to share your story with them, if I can meet with them together?"

"Yes, of course. We appreciate your efforts, Reverend Pierce," Alex K answered as he stood to shake hands again with the reverend.

"If it doesn't get too late in the day, I may stop by your place on my way home tomorrow, if that is okay with you, Mrs. Kammer?" Reverend Pierce nodded towards Suzanah.

"Yes, yes, indeed, Reverend. I will be sure to keep the kettle on and a couple of biscuits ready to warm for you," Suzanah added with a slight smile as she stood next to Alex K.

Izrael jumped to his feet which felt much lighter than they had earlier when they walked to the church. "Thank you, sir, Reverend Pierce! I sure appreciate all that you are doing, sir, Reverend!"

The four chuckled at Izrael's reply as they stepped out of the office, down the stairs outside and said their goodbyes. The walk home had a much better feel to it. In fact, Izrael may have made the walk three or four times longer as he ran circles around his parents, gushing his hope that all the drama may finally be coming to an end.

Suzanah listened and smiled at her son as he gushed, hoping, and praying to herself that his hopes and dreams will indeed come true.

CHAPTER 38

"RESTLESS WAITING"

Izrael awoke the next morning feeling a little sluggish. He had not slept much, thinking too hard about the meeting with Reverend Pierce the day before and the possibilities for relief in the near future. As he walked into the kitchen for breakfast, he was surprised to see Poppa still in the house. He was waiting on Phina and Nikki, as he had offered them a ride to school.

"Phina, sweetheart, your hair looks perfect, come on, I can't wait all day for you," Poppa said while Nikki hung on his arm giggling and hugging Poppa.

"Can I ride along with you, Poppa?" Iz asked, "unless you want me to get started outside, of course."

"Why don't you get started with the smaller animals, Iz, thank you. I will catch up with you when I get back," Poppa answered as he smiled seeing Josephina hurrying to the front door. "I will see you both soon," he added then hurried out the door behind his two youngest daughters.

"Poppa just loves to give those two rides, you know that don't you, Iz?" Momma said smiling while cleaning up behind the girls. "I think they make him feel young," she added giggling.

"Is Poppa going anywhere else, Momma?" Iz asked in a serious tone.

"What do you mean, Iz?" Momma asked puzzled by the question.

"I mean he seemed kind of in a hurry and like he didn't want me to tag along is all, Momma" Iz answered.

"No, no, don't be silly, he's a bit restless, as we all are, Izrael. He is hopeful that Reverend Pierce will bring us good news this afternoon," Momma said as she hugged Izrael from the side. "Now, sit down, son, your breakfast is getting cold."

The rest of the morning went by quickly. Poppa returned directly from taking Phina and Nikki to school, just as Momma said he would. This relieved Izrael greatly. He had still wondered even though Momma reassured him nothing else was going on. The two worked hard side by side. Things seemed normal again, for the moment anyway.

After lunch Poppa and Izrael were working outside of the barn. Poppa had suggested earlier that they stay close enough to the house to hear a vehicle, in the event Reverend Pierce came to visit. He had joked about tea and Momma's biscuits being enough to draw him over, even if he didn't have much news to share. Izrael had laughed with Poppa, but he wanted so much for Reverend Pierce to have good news.

About 2:00 that afternoon they heard a car followed by the sound of a quiet horn. "That must be him," Izrael blurted out.

"Slow down there, buddy! He can wait. Besides, Momma will be getting the tea and biscuits ready, and they will be ready by the time we get inside." Poppa did not want Reverend Pierce to think they were desperate, and Izrael understood clearly.

"You are right, as always, Poppa!" Izrael stated to Poppa. "I agree. Let me finish tying up this rope here. I will meet you inside."

"Very good, Iz. I will head on in and see you there," Poppa answered.

While Izrael finished with the rope and picking up a few tools they would not need later in the afternoon, he reflected on all that had happened over the past several years. He could hardly believe they were still dealing with the same issues. Not much had changed, as far as relationships outside of the family. His thoughts went to his friends; the Four Musketeers. Two, actually three, of them had broken trust in each other. They had promised to always be friends, to go through life together, and to simply share life together. Now, none of it was possible.

Izrael pulled himself together. He was anxious to hear what Reverend Pierce had to say about the birth certificate. He did not want to waste another moment pining away at the past, on all that could have been, or should have been. He hurried down to the house.

As Izrael entered the house, it seemed very quiet, but only for a moment. Soon he heard the booming voice of Reverend Pierce echoing throughout the house.

Iz walked into the kitchen, removing his hat, and extending a greeting to all in the room. He was taught to always greet everyone when you enter a room, and not to wait until those already in the room did the greeting. Poppa always said it was bad manners to enter a room and stand and wait for others to say hello first. Izrael worked hard to remember his manners, always.

"Good afternoon, Reverend Pierce," Izrael spoke first while shaking hands with the reverend who had just taken a bite of his biscuit.

"Come in, son," Momma said to Izrael. "Reverend Pierce was just about to go over some things he learned today."

"Thank you, Momma," Izrael said as he sat down next to Poppa. Momma had already placed a cup of tea and a biscuit for Iz. He felt too anxious to sip or take a bite, so he just sat.

"Nice to see you again, Izrael," Reverend Pierce began. "Yes, I did learn a bit this morning, after visiting with my friend and his brother who just happened to be at the church where my friend pastors. I gave his attorney brother a quick snippet of your situation and he shared some advice. Basically, Izrael, unless Carolina agrees to change the birth certificate, you are stuck."

"What? That's it? What kind of attorney is this guy? Does he not help people?" Izrael felt stumped and, at the same time, furious. "How can she get away with this? Why is it okay to lie about something like this? I don't get it!" Izrael crossed his arms in front of him and pushed his chair back, away from the table.

"The law doesn't seem to do much for the father these days. It's all about what the mother says at this point, according to the attorney." Reverend Pierce added, "but if she agrees to...."

This time Momma interrupted the reverend. "She won't agree, I can tell you that much. She is not interested in who the real father is. She has loved Izrael since high school, and she is not about to stop trying to win him over. This is not the good news we hoped to hear, Reverend Pierce."

Poppa sat forward, leaning on his arms, resting them on the table. "No, sir, it is not good" was all he could say.

Izrael fought tears. He could feel them stinging the corners of his eyes. He refused to let himself get emotional.

"Folks, let me try talking with Carolina and her momma. Maybe I can reason with them." Reverend Pierce seemed to think they could be reasonable people.

"You can try but they won't listen, and they certainly will not go for anything except to concede that Izrael will remain Jane Mae's father, at least on paper." Poppa added, "She knows what she wants, and she won't stop until she has won or at least thinks she has won."

Momma lit up when Poppa said, "at least thinks she has won," but she kept it to herself, for now.

"Again, I am so sorry I did not have better news. I will keep you informed." With that, Reverend Milton Pierce left them feeling doubtful of what the future might hold for Izrael, Carolina and especially for Jane Mae "Kammer."

CHAPTER 39

"JANE MAE"

Over the years since Jane Mae was born, the Kammer family had their share of issues with the Parker family. After much time, and for the most part, the families got along, mostly due to Suzanah and her efforts to keep the peace.

As a baby, Jane Mae mostly cried. While she grew, the crying turned into whining and the whining then to full blown screaming. She was difficult to be around. As much as they had tried through the years, most of the Kammer family now simply avoided her, especially Izrael. He struggled tolerating her sounds. They seemed to make his head spin, to the point he wanted to scream too, although he never did. Izrael could feel his anxiety building.

Suzanah tried many times to talk with Jane Mae. Most efforts were in vain. The moment Suzanah sat down near Jane Mae to attempt to communicate with her, Jane Mae would jump up and begin to skip in circles while chanting her own name over and over. Suzanah found it odd but mostly she found it very sad. She would call out to Jane Mae who would only chant louder.

On this particular day after Suzanah had tried talking with Jane Mae again, she understood more of the words in her chant. She was sure she heard their last name, Kammer. She listened closer and became even more sure. She wasn't sure what to think about that but chose to keep listening.

Suddenly she heard, "Kammer Jane Mae" over and over. She was sure about it. Sure enough she asked Carolina who had been in the house doing some work that Suzanah had agreed to pay her for. Carolina stepped out to the porch to beat on a rug. Suzanah arose from her chair and asked Carolina straight on, "Is she saying 'Kammer Jane Mae' in her chant, Carolina? I have been listening closely and I keep hearing this."

"Oh, I don't know," Carolina answered immediately. "Her chants change every day. I never know from one minute to the next what she might say, Mrs. Kammer." Carolina seemed to brush off Jane Mae's behavior as nothing more than child's play.

Suzanah was not as sure. She wondered if there might be something wrong. She chose not to continue the conversation with Carolina but to take time to pray later. She was sure God would reveal the truth, in His time, and in the right place.

CHAPTER 40

"MOMMA'S NEW THOUGHTS"

After breakfast and the girls having left for school, Momma asked Izrael and Poppa to stay a few minutes to share some thoughts that had come to her after their last visit with Reverend Pierce.

Both agreed and were sitting at the table waiting for Momma to sit with them.

Finally, she sat, and began, "Do you remember, Alexander, after Reverend Pierce told us what he did how you responded? You told the reverend that Carolina won't stop until she has won."

"Yes, I remember saying that Darling," Poppa answered.

"Well you then said, 'at least thinks she has won!'" Momma exclaimed.

After some silence, including Poppa and Izrael looking at each other then back to Momma, she nudged more, "You said 'at least she THINKS she has won" accentuating the word "THINKS."

Both Poppa and Iz seemed to understand at the same time, saying "OH!" at the same time. Then silence again.

"Don't you see? We simply need to convince Carolina that she has won in order to break this curse and move forward without all this pressure on Izrael," Momma continued to explain.

"I think she will break again and stop this nonsense of Izrael being the father on Jane Mae's birth certificate. I believe we can convince her to fix it." Momma smiled as if she had won the lottery.

"And how in the world are we going to convince her of that, Momma?" Izrael could not help feeling skeptical.

"I am so glad you asked, Iz!" Momma went on talking about Jane Mae and the things she had noticed about her. She explained how sad it made her for the child, but it also brought more clarity to her about her behavior. The three talked for another hour or more until Poppa finally announced that their work on the ranch would not fend for itself. He urged Izrael to follow him out and off to get busy. They left Suzanah with her thoughts which she carried out to the porch with her and immediately began to pray. She knew God would guide her and the family, to understand what was next and to continue to pursue the truth.

CHAPTER 41

"IZRAEL'S FRIENDS"

Time continued to pass. Momma stayed focus on getting to the truth of Jane Mae's father. The whole family agreed to continue pursuing the truth, but they seemed to run into one dead end after another.

Priscilla and Lucy shared their concerns with Momma, asking her if she had become too fixated on finding out the truth. Momma assured both of her girls she was fine, but she knew there was more to the story that Carolina shared. She was more determined than ever to uncover the truth among the lies.

Finally, one Sunday after church, while the family was gathered outside, making last minute plans for the afternoon, Carolina, Jane Mae, and Ms. Parker approached the Kammer family.

"We want to talk, can we come to your house?" Carolina stated emphatically.

"Yes, yes, of course. Please do. We have plenty to share. Come right away," Momma answered before anyone else could.

Izrael was stunned. He did not feel right having all the Parkers at their home. He felt sure there was more to this than simply wanting to talk. He was very suspicious.

During the walk home, Izrael continued to ask Momma why she agreed to let the Parker family come to their house for lunch. Momma clearly felt it was time to get things out in the open. She was sure there would be answers today and urged Izrael to be patient and wait. This was not easy for Izrael. He was worried.

After lunch, the younger girls went out to play, including Jane Mae who seemed content playing in the outdoor playhouse. Josephina and Nikki tried to play with her, but Jane Mae mostly kept to herself, chanting a tune they could not understand.

Carolina began talking with the rest of the family. Ms. Parker sat silently away from the table where the rest of the family sat. Everyone listened intently.

"I know you are all upset with all of the gossip recently, and I believe it is time to air all the dirty laundry." Carolina continued with more hints at finally telling the truth until Izrael could not take it any longer. She was doing it again, talking in circles and he just wouldn't listen to her anymore.

Izrael stood and raised his voice louder than he had ever raised it. "Carolina Jane Parker! What is wrong with you? Why don't you just say it? We know you were raped. We know that MJ, Benji and Cliff all had something to do with it and we know you don't want us, or anyone else, to know the truth. But, somehow, some way, the truth will be revealed. The truth is what sets us free, after all! Jesus taught this to His disciples, and it is the only way to truth and light. So, come on! Please!

Just tell us! Quit beating around the bush. Quit the drama and just talk!!"

Priscilla could not resist the urge to applaud. She even stood up and started clapping. Mark was on his way up to join her when Poppa stood.

As soon as Poppa stood up, everyone, including Izrael sat back down.

"Let's all calm down. It's time to take a breath. Let's pray together," Poppa said and began the most eloquent and meaningful prayer he had ever prayed. Everyone in the room had tears in their eyes. Even Ms. Parker felt a tinge of moisture in the corners of her eyes that she had not felt in years.

Carolina was bawling. Her sobs were heard over everyone's responses to Poppa's prayer.

"I already told Mrs. Kammer what happened that day and obviously the rest of you know now so I won't talk about that. What I want to say is that I am sorry for what I have caused this family. Even in the midst of chaos and lies, you still treated me well."

Carolina then turned towards Izrael and said, "Izrael, I have loved you since the first day we met. You were so kind to me. You didn't laugh at me or talk about me behind my back like the rest of the kids. I could tell you were different. I wanted you to love me back, but I went about it the wrong way. I am sorry for all that I have done to you, Izrael. I wish I could take it all back and start over. Maybe we would still be friends." Carolina began to sniffle. This time she did not scream and carry on like she had done before when she cried in front of the family. She simply sat and cried quietly to herself.

No one spoke for a very long time.

Finally, Izrael stood up, walked over to where Carolina sat and said these few words, "Carolina, I forgive you. I am sorry for all you have been through. You did not deserve what happened to you."

Izrael walked out the front door, out to the barn to Mindee, got her ready and took off as fast as he could, far, far *Into the Canyon*. Speedy Iz was quickly out of sight. When they had gotten as far as possible, without going onto someone else's land, Izrael slid down, opened his day pack, and pulled out his journal.

His mind was racing with thoughts of Grandpa K. He wondered over and over in his mind what Grandpa K would have done if he had been here. Would he have applauded Izrael? Would he have said anything to Carolina? It really didn't matter. Grandpa K was not there, and he could never be again. Izrael needed to grow up and take care of things himself. He felt he had done just that by confronting Carolina, and then forgiving her. He could hardly believe he had done that. Of all things, he never thought he would ever forgive her, but he did just that.

What was next? Izrael began to write and write, then write some more. His pencil finally broke after writing for what seemed like hours. He knew it was time to go.

CHAPTER 42

"RELIEF OR NOT?"

Over the next few days things had settled some, but definitely not completely. No one really knew what to say about what had taken place between Carolina and Izrael. Mostly, everyone stopped talking about it and attempted to get to a place of normal, once again.

The uncertainty of Jane Mae's biological father continued to linger but it did not seem as important anymore. The determination to get Izrael's name off her birth certificate also seemed to wane. No one really knew why but the pressure was less and the anxiety and feeling of a dark cloud was gone.

Lucy felt relief for Briella although she could not explain why or how that came to be.

Even Priscilla felt the pressure she put on herself with baking cherry pies lessening a bit.

"Oh, Momma, the county fair is next week!" Priscilla exclaimed to Momma a few days after Carolina, Jane Mae and Ms. Parker had been to Kammer Ranch. Momma smiled, "It will be a fun time won't it Cilla?" was all she said.

Momma kept a few things pondering in her heart. She felt a great relief for Izrael but knew this was not over. She was sure the lies, the arguing and the grief from Carolina and her family would return. She did not know when, she did not know how, but she knew it was coming. Izrael was a kind and loving young man now. He was seeking his own way, and she was sure there would be drama to get through before it could all be over.

CHAPTER 43

"IZRAEL"

"Momma, Poppa, can we talk?" Izrael said firmly while stepping into the family room after his younger sisters had gone to bed.

"Of course, we can, son," Poppa answered, "come, sit."

Izrael sat between his parents in silence for several minutes before he began.

"I have been thinking a lot about Grandpa K lately," Izrael started. He did not look at Poppa, as he was sure he would feel emotional talking about Grandpa K. They had not spoken of him for some time.

"He has been on my mind I think mostly because of all the drama around Carolina and Jane Mae. I have wondered how he would have handled things, if he would support me now, and what wisdom he might share with me. Then it occurred to me. I have you, Poppa. You are the next generation of Grandpa K. You continue to impart your wisdom to me, and I would have it no other way. The generations continue on with the last one leaving a trail for those of us they left behind to follow." Izrael paused. "It will be my turn next, Poppa, Momma. Someone will expect me to lead them and guide them with the wisdom

I have learned from you and from my grandparents before you. I want to learn more so that I can get it right."

Iz heard Momma sniffle as he continued.

"I have an idea I want to share with you, something I think that will help me grow more," Izrael added.

Momma dabbed her eyes with a tissue but didn't speak. No one said a word until Izrael began again.

"I would like to go spend some time with Grandma K and Aunt K, Poppa. They have been on my mind a lot too. I have wondered often how they have done without Grandpa K all these years. I know they are strong women, but Grandma K is up there in years now. I am sure they could use some help around the house and property. I could also use a change of pace, a change of scenery and especially a change of drama." Izrael managed a small chuckle which made both Momma and Poppa chuckle with him.

"I am not surprised by any of this, Izrael," Poppa finally said after a few more minutes of silence. "The last few years have been difficult, to say the least. I have worried about you and wondered if we might need to give you some time to recover. A few weeks on the other side of the mountain will be good for you. What do you think, Momma?"

Momma had continued to remain silent. The thought of her only son not being on the ranch day after day was a little hard to swallow. However, knowing he was taking care of other family members was heartwarming at the same time. "I think it is a perfect idea!" Momma finally said. A tinge of sadness could be heard in her voice which made Izrael's throat tighten. He could never be away from Momma for long.

"My future plans are not changing, Momma. I still have every intention of continuing Kammer Ranch with Poppa. I will only stay a few weeks. I plan to get back before it freezes, well before the first freeze." Izrael stated emphatically.

"I sure like the idea of your returning before the freeze, Iz!" Poppa said immediately. "There is so much to do to prepare for the winter months. Grandma K and Aunt K will definitely appreciate what you can do for them to prepare also. This is a great plan, Izrael. Thank you for looking out for my momma and sister. They will be so happy to see you. Now let's plan your trip over the mountain. It definitely won't be as hard of a trip as you and I made the winter we lost Grandpa K."

"Yes, sir. I agree and thank you both. I love you both so much," Izrael said feeling the lump in his throat grow tighter.

CHAPTER 44

"TRAVELING"

Izrael spent much time preparing for this trip. He could hardly believe he was actually on his way, alone this time, over the mountain to see Grandma K and Aunt K. He was eager to get to work on their place although he realized it was much smaller than Kammer Ranch so it would be much different.

Aunt K spent much of her time growing and tending a garden. The produce kept them fed throughout the winter and the sales from the produce kept their finances intact just enough to get by, as Aunt K always told Poppa.

Izrael would use his time making sure the ground was ready for the winter months. He was sure there would be plenty to keep him occupied. He was excited to get to help and get away from certain things at home.

His journey began, riding on Mindee as before. Iz thought of Momma and his sisters. He knew Poppa was more than able to take care of everyone. Lucy and Priscilla's husbands were also close by. Still, the thought of not being there made him feel sad. He had not felt this kind of sadness before; the inability to be in two places at the same time was more difficult than he imagined.

He knew the time would go by quickly and soon he would be home again, managing the same chores and working with Poppa.

All these thoughts in Izrael's head made the ride over the mountain go by quickly. While he and Poppa rode two days in the middle of winter, Izrael was able to get over in one full day. He would arrive by suppertime. Izrael was glad to not spend an overnight in the middle of the mountains alone. He was sure it would have been harder without Poppa.

Momma packed him plenty of snacks and he had enough water to travel at least 3 days.

Even with being so very well prepared, Iz was thrilled to see Aunt K's house as he cleared the top of the last ridge. The ride down would still take time, but seeing the house gave him great relief.

As Izrael made his way down the mountainside, thoughts of riding through mountain roads flashed through his mind. He tried to keep the more difficult memories from entering his mind, but it was difficult. "Maybe this ride will flush those memories out, Mindee, what do you think girl?" Iz said out loud as he patted Mindee's neck. Mindee responded with her usual snorts that always gave Iz the sense she was truly listening. The long day of riding had given Izrael the space to say whatever he wanted, to let the feelings out and to clear his mind. He felt some relief.

His thoughts turned quickly to Grandma K and Aunt K as he heard a voice in the distance and could see Aunt K waving a cloth in the air to welcome him. Iz pressed into Mindee enough to get her started into a gallop. They sped up even more when he saw Grandma K stepping in behind Aunt K. Soon they were at the house, being hugged and welcomed as only a loving

Grandma and Aunt would and could do. Izrael felt the warmth and the affection. He was very glad to be here.

"Come, let's get you inside and cleaned up," Aunt K offered. "We have some dinner about ready. I bet you are hungry, aren't you, Iz?"

"Yes, yes, indeed. I am very hungry, thank you, Aunt K," Iz replied while squeezing Grandma K's hand as they walked into the house.

Everything was the same as he had remembered. It was as though nothing had changed, and Grandpa K was still in the back bedroom. The kitchen, the sitting room, everything looked the same.

"Some things never change!" Izrael announced as they walked into the house, "and I'm so grateful!" Izrael added.

The three giggled as they settled Izrael in. He went to clean up and was delighted to find all his favorites that Aunt K and Grandma K remembered him loving to eat, set out on the table.

"Who is going to help us eat all this food?" Izrael said as he walked into the kitchen. "I should have brought the girls with me to help us!"

Dinner was exceptional. Iz did not waste a minute complimenting the chefs. The remainder of the evening was spent catching up, although Izrael did not give too much information about Carolina and Jane Mae. He would save that for another day when they had plenty of time to talk. He was eager to get Grandma K's opinion and advice. Next to Grandpa K, he knew she would give him the right kind of advice he needed right now.

CHAPTER 45

"TIME WELL SPENT"

The days and weeks went by quickly, as Izrael had expected they would. He and Poppa worked out a plan for what day he would return to Kammer Ranch. He made sure Aunt K and Grandma K were fully aware of his plans. They planned out each day together, making sure to cover all that was needed in preparation for the winter. Aunt K's home sat on the side of the mountain that received more snow. Their winters were spent mostly indoors so stocking up and having enough was of utmost importance. Izrael learned a lot from his aunt and grandma. He was so pleased to have taken this opportunity to help them. In fact, he told them both he would make it a regular event, to come back and help every fall. This pleased Aunt K and Grandma K so much that a little moisture filled their eyes when Izrael made this promise.

It was one week before Izrael was set to travel back home. Grandma K asked Izrael to sit and talk. It was just the two of them. Aunt K had taken the list they made the night before to town to shop. It would be her last shopping trip for several weeks; she would be gone a good long while that day.

Grandma K began, "We have sure enjoyed having you here with us, Izrael Shane Kammer. You are such a blessing to me and your aunt. Thank you for choosing to spend time with us and helping us prepare for another winter. Now I want to spend a little time talking about you. I know we have talked a little, but I want to ask you a hard question and I want you to feel comfortable sharing with me. It's not like I can go anywhere and tell anyone else about any of it." The two laughed quietly together over Grandma K's last statement.

"What would you like to know that I haven't already told you, Grandma K?" Izrael questioned. "I told you how things were with Carolina and her daughter, Jane Mae. I told you about her momma and all the drama they tried to create, and I told you about the birth certificate. I feel pretty stuck when it comes to that piece of paper, I have to admit."

"That's what I want to ask you, Izrael. What do you plan to do about that birth certificate?" Grandma K asked pointedly.

"What do you mean, Grandma K? There isn't anything I can do about it," Izrael answered weakly.

"Think again, grandson. Think hard. I want you to take a minute and imagine yourself as the one who had a birth certificate with a man's name on that is not your own poppa. Think how that would make you feel, Izrael." Grandma K ended with some hard things for Izrael to consider.

They sat in quiet for some time. Grandma K got up from the table a few times to check the woodburning stove and to freshen the hot water in their tea. Izrael noticed how much slower Grandma K moved, but he had not mentioned it. He was almost afraid to think of what was next for Grandma K.

"I don't move as fast as I used to do I, Izrael?" Grandma K said as she sat back down. How Grandma K always seemed to know what Iz was thinking still surprised him.

"How?" Izrael started, then shook his head, "never mind. I know." Izrael said while giggling. This made Grandma K giggle too.

"Let's not distract ourselves from my question, Izrael" Grandma K got them back on track and focused.

"I won't, Grandma K, don't worry," Iz quickly answered. "I have actually given this a lot of thought, even before I came here, Grandma K. It makes me feel sad for Jane Mae every time I think of it. I want her to know her daddy and it is very unfair for her not to. I believe I am going to have to confront those so-called friends of mine about what happened to Carolina."

"How will you do that, Izrael?" Grandma K asked.

"Well, I have heard MJ's side of the story. It's time I talk with the other two. If I can get them each alone that will be ideal, but they don't do much separately, Grandma K. It's kind of strange how they are," he finished.

"I am sure you will find a way to talk with those two young men. It is honorable that you want to help Carolina and Jane Mae after all that has happened." Grandma K added.

"You know, it's not about Carolina anymore, Grandma K. It's about the child, Jane Mae. She needs a poppa," Izrael stated and realized for the first time that there truly was something he could do to help Jane Mae. "I will keep working on this, Grandma K, I promise. I will make sure the child has a daddy."

"That is wonderful, Izrael. I am very proud of you. I hope you will write to me once you have resolved these things." Grandma K added as she patted Izrael's hand. Then she said one more beautiful statement to her grandson, "Izrael Shane, as you go through this process, remember there is one thing you need to do for YOU, grandson."

"What one thing, Grandma K?" Iz asked.

"To clear your mind and find your soul," Grandma K said softly then hugged Izrael with the kind of grandma hug that left a soul feeling warm, for a very long time.

CHAPTER 46

"WELCOME HOME"

The ride home was even faster than the ride over the mountain to Aunt K's house. Izrael knew he and Mindee were moving with more speed, as they had both gotten home sick during their trip. Izrael was thankful for the time he got to spend with Grandma K and Aunt K, but he missed Momma and Poppa so much, not to mention all of his sisters and that sweet little baby Briella. He could hardly wait to see everyone.

He made it home by suppertime which had been his plan all along. As he neared the house, he noticed the extra cars out front and knew Lucy and Priscilla were there along with their spouses and the baby! This made his heartbeat quicken as he pressed into Mindee to go faster. Mindee galloped quickly to the barn. Izrael noticed right away the barn doors were open.

As they turned the corner, they heard a loud, "SURPRISE!"

The whole family was in the barn! Iz could hardly believe it. All day he had imagined walking into the house with the aromas of fresh biscuits and cherry pie. He certainly did not expect to find everyone in the barn! Izrael laughed out loud, while the corners of his eyes moistened as he slid down Mindee's side.

Priscilla's husband, Mark, stepped in and took Mindee so Iz would be free to give hugs. Momma was first. She hugged Izrael so tight his hat fell off. Iz could not help but notice the tears going down her cheeks and felt the moistness on the side of his face.

"I'm sorry, Momma. I did not mean to make you worry about me," Izrael whispered.

"Oh, no, Izrael, these are just happy tears. I am so happy to have you home. I am very proud of what you did, going over to help your aunt and grandma." Momma made sure to explain her tears.

The hugs and pats on his back kept going all the way to the house. Izrael thought to himself how he had never felt so loved in all of his life. He hoped the same for everyone. Even Carolina and Jane Mae. Izrael almost smacked himself on the back of his head for almost ruining the moment. He wanted to enjoy the time with his family as he literally shook their two names right out of his thoughts.

"Guess what you missed, Bubba?" Josephina interrupted Izrael's thoughts.

"What? What did I miss, Phina?" Iz shot back as he turned, throwing his arm around Josephina's waist, and spinning her in the air.

Josephina squealed with delight as Nikola quickly jumped in to get her turn with Iz.

"You missed the County Fair!" Josephina laughed and shouted over Nikki's giggles.

"Oh, that's right! How was it? How were the pies?" Izrael immediately turned towards Priscilla who was beaming with delight.

"I won the pie contest, Iz, can you believe it? I still can't and it was several weeks ago," Cilla added as she giggled along with her little sisters.

They all cheered for Priscilla at the same time which made everyone laugh. Their voices were so loud they could be heard across the valley.

This made Alex K and Suzanah smile. They followed their family, hand in hand, their hearts swelling as they made their way back to the house. All was good. Izrael was home.

The rest of the evening was spent mostly eating and laughing. Izrael had plenty of time to share stories about what he had been doing while at Aunt K's house, how she and Grandma K were doing and everything in between.

CHAPTER 47

"WHAT PLANS?"

Izrael felt truly happy to be home. Every morning when he awoke, he prayed a prayer of praise for being where he was and with the people he loved most. Iz was determined to never take anything for granted.

A few weeks had passed since he had his talk with Grandma K. He tried a few times to get in touch with Benji and Cliff but gave up after several attempts. On this particular Saturday morning Iz decided it was time to get busy again. When he walked into the kitchen, he did not find Momma. He wondered where she was when he heard voices coming from the front porch.

Iz walked out the front door and was almost shocked to see both Benji and Cliff as well as MJ standing down just below the porch. Momma and Poppa were sitting in their porch chairs talking with the guys. Everyone turned towards the door as Iz stepped out.

"Good afternoon, sleepyhead!" MJ shot out.

"It's hardly anywhere near afternoon, MJ" Izrael shot back quickly as he hurried down the stairs to the three guys Iz had always considered his best friends. His mind was racing, knowing how much they had betrayed him.

"Where have you guys been the last few months?" Izrael asked in a strong and somewhat serious tone.

"What do you mean, Iz? We've all been working and staying busy with our own families!" Cliff answered before anyone else could, shuffling his feet in the dirt nervously.

Izrael turned to look up at Momma and Poppa, who were still seated in their chairs on the porch. "Do you mind if I take the guys up to the barn and we hang out there for a little while, Poppa?"

"Sure, of course, Iz. We are pretty caught up on things. I know you 4 have much to catch up on." Poppa answered, adding "We will need to do a few things before lunch so don't be too long."

"Yes sir, we won't be long, thank you, sir," Izrael answered.

All 3 guys waved to Izrael's Momma and Poppa as they hurried around the house and over to the barn. Iz had talked with Momma and Poppa about his conversation with Grandma K. They were very supportive of his hopes and plans to get the right name on Jane Mae's birth certificate.

When Izrael rolled open the heavy barn doors, he could hear Mindee's happy neigh welcoming them in. The other horses made similar sounds and leaned over their stall doors while the boys all stepped inside. The cold wind pushed them into the barn, providing a safe and warmer space to talk.

"So, what's up, Speedy Iz?" MJ shot out. "You seem very serious right now."

"I haven't been called Speedy Iz for some time, you know?" Iz answered as he began to lean on a pile of hay nearby. The guys all followed and found a place to sit.

Izrael started. "A lot has happened in the last several years since we graduated from high school, guys. Life is a lot more serious now, and we have to make important decisions about the future. Do you know what I mean?"

"I do!" Cliff piped in immediately. "My poppa keeps telling me I need to get things together and act more like a man." Cliff started to laugh when he caught Benji's look and stopped.

"This is serious, guys. We aren't the Four Musketeers anymore. We are all men now." Izrael said about as flatly and firmly as he could manage.

Several minutes of silence followed. Finally, MJ spoke.

"I know what you mean, Izrael," MJ responded. "Life is changing and you're right, we are all men now. No longer silly boys acting out and teasing each other." MJ's look on his face was almost painfully serious. The silence lingered again.

"So what's the big deal?" Benji nearly yelled this time. "I mean, okay, we aren't boys now, we are men, so what? Why are we talking about this? I don't get it."

Benji quickly stood up, appearing ready to leave when Cliff stepped in next to him. "I think what we need to do here is finally come clean on some things, Benji. A lot of things have changed for us Four Musketeers alright. Most of that is our fault, and it's time we admit it and try to move on."

MJ and Izrael hardly moved. Neither said a word, staying silent, listening, and hoping the silence would help heal and bring out the truth.

Benji sat again. This time he sat all the way down in the dirt, between two bales of hay. Only the top of his head was visible. Izrael was sure he saw tears begin to creep down the side of Benji's cheek. He knew better than to interrupt what was finally beginning to unfold. He could hardly believe it. Iz felt nervousness building in his innermost being.

Cliff walked over near Benji, his eyes looking down on his friend. The two were truly like brothers, nearly as close as twins. At times in the past it appeared they breathed in unison. They would complete each other's sentences and cover each other's mishaps. This time a deep sadness filled the barn. They were both now openly crying.

Izrael was the first to speak next. MJ stepped out closer to the doors. The look on his face was of deep disappointment. Izrael spoke clearly, "Whatever you have to say guys, remember what we learned in church as kids. The truth sets us free. No matter what."

The tension eased slightly. Cliff's and Benji's breathing in unison had quieted and even sounded like they were breathing separately. In any other situation, Iz may have found it humorous. Not this time. The silence lingered, becoming more deafening.

Finally, Benji's words began and broke the silence. "Everything from that day is a blur to me. It always has been, even right after it was over."

Cliff nodded, profusely, in agreement.

One after the other, Benji and Cliff replayed the event, out loud, to the two other Musketeers.

Benji continued, "It really started out as a game. We didn't mean to scare her."

"No, that's right! We were teasing her, trying to get her to jump in the truck," Cliff added immediately.

"All of a sudden, I don't remember how or why, we were chasing her," Benji rushed his words.

"Running, fast. She was so fast!" Cliff's breathing got deeper and faster as if he was running after Carolina at that very moment.

"She turned, running into the bushes. Not sure why she did that, do you remember that MJ?" Benji turned to MJ who had been pacing back and forth in front of the barn doors as the two spoke back and forth, his head shaking to the rhythm of their words.

"Oh, yeah, MJ was there! Of course he was there, Benji, he was driving the pickup!" Cliff almost yelled out as he switched his weight back and forth from one foot to the other, as if dancing to a wild beat of a drum.

Izrael felt sick to his stomach listening to each retell what he envisioned when MJ shared with him, although something felt different than what MJ described. Izrael was not sure what it was, but he stayed focused on Benji's and Cliff's words. The more they talked, the more anxious Iz became, feeling heat swelling up inside him. He had no words to say. He just wanted to scream and rush at both of them.

MJ beat him to it. Before Iz knew what was happening, MJ grabbed a hold of Benji's shirt and pulled him straight up to standing. He was about to punch Benji when Cliff jumped onto MJ's back, knocking him right off his feet.

Iz felt confusion. He was sure he heard MJ say something to Benji, but it was too hard to process in the midst of the intense chaos of the moment.

For the first time ever, the Four Musketeers were fighting. Truly fighting, punches flying in every direction while dirt clouds filled the barn. Even the horses in the stalls were kicking up dirt from all the commotion.

Izrael could take no more. He rushed forward yelling, "Stop it! Stop fighting! What's wrong with you guys? You are friends! Stop fighting, do you hear me? Stop it!"

With Izrael's last words still bouncing off the barn walls, the scuffle screeched to a stop when the doors flung open. Iz looked to see Poppa at the entrance of the barn.

"WHAT IS GOING ON IN HERE, IZRAEL SHANE KAMMER?" Poppa yelled out, louder and in a deeper tone than Izrael ever remembered hearing Poppa.

MJ, Cliff and Benji all jumped to their feet, grabbing their hats, and scrambling to straighten their shirts, tucking in where shirt tails had slipped out. The loose dirt on the ground created a dark cloud, still lingering from the scuffle.

"I asked you a question, Izrael. What is going on in here?" Poppa demanded again, this time not as loudly.

"Sorry, sir, Poppa, so sorry," Iz stammered, feeling embarrassed and a bit disheveled even though he had not been in the middle of the dog pile.

"It's our fault, Mr. Kammer," Cliff jumped in. "Benji and I, well, we got a little rough and..."

"Alright, get yourselves back to your own family ranches and, Izrael, you need to get to work too," Poppa stated firmly. Izrael nodded firmly back, towards Poppa.

"Yes, sir, thank you, sir," MJ answered as he hurriedly pushed the other two out the open barn doors, down the short walkway and to their pickup trucks they had parked in the lower part of the driveway. Another dark cloud of dirt built. Izrael watched it billow up then slowly diminish as the Three (of the Four) Musketeers' words echoed behind them. Words Iz would not easily forget.

Something else bothered Izrael. It was MJ's reaction towards Benji. He wondered why MJ grabbed Benji like he did. Why did he threaten him not to say it? What was Benji going to say? Was there something more to MJ's reaction? Iz felt the need to shake his head, to let it go, but he could not shake off the uneasiness he was feeling about MJ.

His thoughts turned to Carolina. She was no longer his friend; he wanted nothing more to do with her, but he felt sadness for what she had been through, and even more for Jane Mae.

CHAPTER 48

"NOW WHAT?"

The next day Izrael felt the exhaustion in every part of himself; physically, mentally, and emotionally. The event from the day before left him completely unsure of what to do next. He was sure Poppa told Momma all about it. He could hear their soft voices from his bedroom last night but had been too wiped out to even try to listen.

Momma gave him a warm hug and a comforting breakfast to start the day. Everyone was getting ready for church. Izrael hurried to catch up.

It was an uneventful morning, one everyone seemed to be thankful for. After church the family shared their usual Sunday meal. The conversation around the table was polite but a bit tense and unsettled. Izrael had a strong feeling they all knew about the Four Musketeers coming apart the day before. He wasn't sure so he did not mention anything. No one did. Until after the kitchen was cleaned up.

Izrael and all the family gathered in the family room. The room felt a little smaller since Lucy and Priscilla's husbands joined the family, but still provided a comfortable space to gather. The initial silence held a sense of comfort, broken only by Briella's soft coos and giggles. It was a peaceful and safe place to be. Izrael did not want it to end.

Poppa spoke first. "How are you feeling today, son?"

"I'm, well, I feel, to be honest, Poppa, I am exhausted and not sure what to do next," Izrael answered with a tone of exasperation and fatigue.

Momma's eyes moistened but her voice was strong. "We understand that, Izrael. You had a hard day with your friends yesterday."

"I don't want to call them friends anymore, Momma," Iz replied quietly.

More silence in the room. Lucy stood to carry Briella back to a bedroom after she had fallen asleep in her arms.

The family felt Izrael's pain and stress. Several comments and questions started around the room with the girls all sounding very worried.

"What should we do?"

"What kind of plan do we need now?"

"How can we help you, Iz?"

The last question came from Izrael's youngest sister, Nikola. Iz had hardly realized how grown up she was becoming. He always noticed how smart Nikki was, but she was changing and understanding things the family always protected her from in the past.

"You sound so grown up, Nik," Iz said almost playfully. Nobody felt very playful.

"I am growing up, Bubba! I worry about you, and I can't help but worry about Jane Mae. She is the one who will suffer the most from all this." Nikola surprised everyone with her last statement.

Nikki was sitting next to Momma who put her arm lovingly around her daughter, pulling her close after her thoughtful comments. Momma leaned in and whispered to her youngest child, "You are very special, my love" then kissing her softly on the top of her head.

Everyone felt the tenderness slowly replace the stressfulness. Momma prayed quietly, then out loud while the family one by one bowed their heads in reverence.

Poppa closed the family meeting, "Momma, Izrael and I will pay a visit to Reverend Pierce tomorrow."

CHAPTER 49

"FIXING THINGS"

Mondays always came quickly after all the family time over the weekends. On this particular Monday Izrael felt mixed emotions of hopefulness and worry. He wondered which would win out and take over.

Once Josephina and Nikola were at school, Momma and Poppa sat down with Izrael to plan for their meeting with the reverend.

"Now that we have a better idea about Jane Mae's biological father, son, we want to talk with Reverend Pierce. Remember, he offered to help us with the birth certificate. Let's see what the reverend is really made of." Poppa explained to Iz.

Momma gave Poppa a little bit of a side-eye look after his last statement. "Be nice, Alexander. He said he would try to help. Let's hope for the best." Momma always looked for the best in everyone.

Izrael smiled. Once again, he felt the enormous support from his family. It meant everything.

As the three neared the entry doors to the church, Reverend Pierce's voice came booming out to greet them.

"Hello Kammer Family! This is a pleasant surprise! What can I do for you on this beautiful Monday? What's on your minds?"

The sound of Reverend Pierce's voice made Izrael jump. Did he see them coming? Iz wondered silently.

"We have some information to discuss with you, Reverend Pierce. Can we come in and talk?" Poppa asked politely.

"Why, yes, of course, Mr. Kammer. I always have time for you and your family, sir. Come on in!" Reverend Pierce welcomed the three as he ushered them through the empty sanctuary again back to his little office. Iz noticed the secretary was not at her desk, not that it mattered to anyone.

Once in Reverend Pierce's office, he invited them to sit and closed the door behind them. Izrael noticed the same old metal chair he had sat in before and quickly set it next to Poppa.

"Now, what can I do for you?" Reverend Pierce said from behind the large wooden desk, clasping his hands, then leaning back in his over-sized chair.

"Will you pray for us first, Reverend Pierce?" Momma asked. After a quick nod from Reverend Pierce, and a short prayer, they began explaining to him why they were there.

"I see," Reverend Pierce assumed the same position he had been in before bowing for the prayer. He slowly rubbed his chin, turned towards a small window, and stared out at the trees close by. Several minutes passed then finally he started, "Hmmm, two boys are involved? I'm not really sure how to know which is the father of the little girl, folks. This is a very difficult situation, and one I am not qualified to help with."

Izrael's face sunk. He had gone with high hopes. He didn't speak but Reverend Pierce noticed his expression.

"I didn't say I won't try to help, son. I said I am not qualified. What I can do is help you find someone who actually is qualified to help. I believe we may need to speak with a medical specialist, folks." Reverend Pierce finished with a deep breath that ended with a snort.

Iz almost chuckled. Instead, he turned towards Momma who looked concerned. She spoke up, "What kind of medical specialist can help us, Reverend Pierce?"

"Well, the kind who help women deliver babies, ma'am," the reverend answered in a much more subdued tone as his face turned a pale shade of pink.

"I see," Poppa added. "Do you happen to know one, sir? Reverend Pierce?"

"Not personally, no, but remember my pastor friend's brother who lives and works in the big city? I have a feeling he has clients who work in the medical field." Reverend Pierce cleared his throat and added, "Let me give him a call. Do you have a few minutes while I step out and call him?"

"Yes, yes, we do, thank you, Reverend Pierce," Poppa answered.

The three waited quietly, for several long minutes.

Izrael's thoughts returned to the event in the barn, the day before, with his now ex-friends. He was still worried about his suspicions around MJ and how he reacted to Benji.

"We are in luck!" Reverend Pierce announced as he loudly stomped back into his office.

Izrael jumped again at the sound of Reverend Pierce's booming voice that immediately interrupted his thoughts, although he was grateful for the interruption.

"My pastor friend's brother just happens to be friends with a one of those doctors who helps deliver babies. He said he would give him a call and find out what can be done. I think between a lawyer and a doctor, we might just get some answers, what do you think folks?" Reverend Pierce smiled as he sat, looking pleased with the information he had for the Kammer's.

"How soon will he know something?" Poppa asked.

"He wasn't sure, Mr. Kammer, but he promised to call me as soon as possible," Reverend Pierce replied quickly.

"We sure can't ask for more than this. Thank you, Reverend Pierce. Your kindness means a lot to the whole Kammer family." Poppa shook hands with the reverend. Poppa, Momma and Iz hurried back down the long hallway and through the empty sanctuary to the front doors.

When they reached the bottom of the stairs, Iz let out a loud sigh of relief. Momma giggled quietly. As they walked back home, they felt a little hope. Poppa warned Iz not to get ahead of himself with excitement, as anything could happen. If Izrael had not learned anything else in the past few years, it was to not expect too much. He had learned patience and how to wait. He was not very good at it, but he knew he had no choice.

CHAPTER 50

"SMALL GLIMPSES"

As the days and weeks passed, life seemed to get back into a routine, for the most part. It did not take much to create anxiety in Iz, with the looming hope of truth dangling in front of him. Every time he heard a vehicle on the road, Iz hurried to see who it was, always hoping to see the reverend's car. Most days the cars simply drove on by Kammer Ranch.

On a cold and windy Friday afternoon, finally Reverend Pierce came for another visit.

"Welcome, Reverend Pierce, please come in from the cold," Suzanah ushered the pastor into the house. Reverend Pierce hurried to stand near the stove which crackled and popped from the hot embers and logs inside.

"It sure feels nice and warm inside your home, Mrs. Kammer. It is a cold, bitter day out there!" the pastor exclaimed.

"Yes, it sure is a cold day, Pastor, it sure is," Momma answered quietly as she hurried to start heating water for tea and gathering biscuits and jelly. "Please, have a seat. Alex K and Izrael should be right along. I am sure they saw you. They aren't working far."

"Thank you, Mrs. Kammer," Reverend Pierce answered as he pulled a chair back from the family table.

While he sat, he heard the front door. Izrael was breathing hard from hurrying down the hill after he saw the reverend parking his car. Poppa was close behind him.

"Come, sit down, you two. I have tea and biscuits about ready," Momma warmly invited her two men to the table.

"Well, I have news. It's not great but it is news," Reverend Pierce began immediately. "My friend's brother talked with the doctor and there is a medical test that can help identify which of the two boys is the father of that little girl."

"The not-so-great-part of this is that both boys have to agree to the test," Reverend Pierce added after taking a big bite of his first biscuit followed by several sips of his tea. He then wiped his mouth with the napkin lying beside his plate and added, "Carolina will also need to agree to a test on her daughter."

"Well, that will never happen!" Izrael blurted out as he leaned back in his chair almost tilting back far enough to fall backwards. Izrael started to stand, feeling an urge to leave the kitchen when Poppa stopped him.

"Izrael Shane Kammer, take a deep breath and hold your tongue son," Poppa spoke sternly. Iz sat and nodded immediately.

"What do you think, Reverend Pierce? Is it even possible to get them all to agree to the test?" Poppa's face looked concerned.

"You know them better than I do, Mr. Kammer, Mrs. Kammer; what do you think?" Reverend Pierce answered right back.

Silence. It said it all. Izrael turned away, looking down the hallway in the house, towards the bedrooms. The only thought in his mind was the same question, "How can we possibly get Benji and Cliff to agree to this test, not to mention Carolina?"

Momma's answer snapped Iz back into the room. For a moment he wondered if he had said his thought out loud.

"It is hard to predict, Reverend Pierce, but we are not ready to give up." Momma was always the optimist. Izrael's spirit smiled broadly, but he kept his expression neutral. He knew not to show excitement.

"Thank you for all your help, Pastor Pierce, we are very grateful for you," Poppa said extending his hand with a warm handshake as he stood. "We will see what happens next," Poppa added.

"Time will tell, Iz, time will tell. The truth eventually comes out, one way or another. Remember the lessons you have learned and how the truth sets us free. Those boys need to be set free from their lies. I can only imagine what they have been going through since that day, Izrael. I can only imagine." Reverend Pierce's voice trailed off as Izrael tried not to relive the afternoon when Benji and Cliff spilled their guts. It was too much to go through once, let alone over and over in his mind.

"Don't let your mind be your worst enemy, son," Reverend Pierce said as he laid a hand on Izrael's left shoulder and winked.

"Yes, sir. Thank you, sir," was all Izrael could say. He looked over at Momma who had a peaceful and calm look on her face along with a loving gentle smile. At that moment Izrael knew nothing else mattered. Life would move on, whether the truth was revealed or not. The best part of all was that everyone knew he truly had nothing to do with Carolina and Jane Mae, and that he had given his all to help discover the truth.

"Jane Mae!" Izrael said out loud.

"Yes," Momma answered, as if to know what he was thinking, and she did. Always.

CHAPTER 51

"BABY BRIELLA"

It was Sunday afternoon again. The whole family went to church together earlier and were gathered at Kammer Ranch for their usual Sunday dinner. The house was filled with quiet chatter while a calm feeling of peace filled the air. Scents of fresh bread baking, chicken roasting and potatoes boiling seemed to compete with the peacefulness. Izrael didn't mind the competition. His stomach was rumbling, and his mind was racing, realizing his own internal competition overwhelming him.

"There you are!" Lucy chimed into his thoughts. "I have been looking for you."

"Is it time to eat?" Iz started to jump to his feet eagerly.

"Almost, Iz," Lucy giggled, "but I wanted to talk with you before we sit down to eat. I realized something this morning, and I want to share it with you first before we all talk today."

"Sure, Lucy. What's on your mind?" Izrael sat next to Lucy in the family room.

"Well, of course you remember us all having such a dark feeling of gloom that somehow had to do with Briella and Jane Mae, right?" Lucy started.

Iz nodded while Lucy continued. "It seems to be gone, Iz. Suddenly it's just gone. I don't know how to explain it, but I think it's gone!"

Izrael paused before responding to Lucy. He had not realized it, having been so deep into the most recent events with his so-called friends. As Lucy spoke, the feeling in the air became even more peaceful and calm.

"Wow, Lucy! I think you're right! I had not noticed but as you said this to me, it felt like the dark cloud separated and was replaced with peace. How amazing is that, Lucy?" Izrael could hardly believe even what he was saying.

"Where is Briella now, Lucy? I want to see her!" Izrael exclaimed excitedly.

"She's still sleeping, Iz. She should be awake from her afternoon nap soon. She will be hungry," Lucy added smiling.

"Just like her Uncle Iz!" Izrael could not help jumping to his feet while he grabbed Lucy's hand and rushed to the kitchen. "It sure smells good in here, Momma, I'm famished!" Izrael felt a rush of joy and happiness. He hardly recognized these emotions. It seemed to have been a very long time since he felt this way.

"Why are you so happy, Iz?" Priscilla turned looking back and forth from Izrael to Lucy. "Hey, you're both smiling, what is going on?" she asked again.

"It's gone, Cilla! The dark cloud, or feeling, or whatever you want to call it, of gloom is gone!" Lucy announced to everyone in the kitchen.

"Really? It's gone?" Priscilla almost sounded skeptical.

"Yay, it's gone!" Josephina and Nikola chanted together taking hands and turning in a circle.

"Let's not get ahead of ourselves, girls. Now, would one of you explain what you are talking about?" Momma demanded, smiling, and wiping her hands on the towel tucked into her waist.

"What is all the commotion about?" Poppa said loudly, adding how he could hear the chatter and laughter all the way down the hall.

More laughter followed until the whole house seemed to swell and shimmy with the sounds. Lucy disappeared when she thought she heard Briella cooing down the hallway. Frank had already retrieved her and was walking towards the kitchen before she could reach the bedrooms. "What's all the noise, Lucy?" Frank asked.

"Oh, the most wonderful news, Frank, come, let's join everyone in the kitchen," Lucy answered while holding tightly to Frank's arm underneath their beautiful Briella.

By the time they stepped back into the kitchen, everyone was making their way to the table where lovely puffs of steam danced from the center of the large table. In fact, everything, and everyone, seemed to be dancing.

Frank settled Briella into her highchair. She could almost sit by herself. Lucy learned if she stuffed Briella's favorite blanket behind her, she would sit easily and not slide to one side or the other. She and Frank sat on each side of Briella. As they settled in, they realized everyone was watching them, or more specifically, they were watching Briella.

"She's perfect, Lucy, Frank. She's truly perfect," Iz said through breaths that seemed to speak on their own.

"Yes, she is" and "So perfect" and "Agree" and "Oohhs" and "Ahhs" followed from each family member.

"Okay, what gives, family?" Frank could not wait another minute to know first of all, why everyone was suddenly so happy and what it had to do with his pretty little baby girl.

Lucy jumped in, "I haven't had a chance to tell Frank what Iz and I talked about. The evidence that has followed took my breath away. I almost have no words. Momma, will you explain?"

"Yes, yes, of course, my darling. I would love to," Momma quickly and eagerly replied.

"You see, Frank, and all the family, as we all know, we have been under a dark cloud of gloom for months now. Specifically, this gloom has hovered over our precious and beautiful Briella. It has been enough gloom to really keep us from talking about it, for fear it would get worse." Momma stopped to take a breath and dab at a tear that started to drop to her cheek.

"Secrets and lies have been a part of the Kammer and Parker families for several years. The lies have haunted all of us at one time or another. Even baby Briella was impacted by the lies. As we have discussed, we all felt that dark impending feeling of gloom and it seemed connected to Briella and Jane Mae. It was a truly fearful feeling. There almost seemed to be a curse working hard to force its' way into our lives, focused on beautiful Briella Suzanah."

"What Lucy discovered this morning and has shared with us now is that the dark cloud has lifted. It's gone. We have nothing to fear. It has been lifted by God's promise that the truth will set us free. Even though it was not our truth to tell, the secrets and lies reached every part of our family, even little Briella," Momma continued.

Gasps and sounds filled the room.

"Thank you, Momma. I could never have said it so perfectly," Lucy whispered to Momma.

"What wonderful joy we have found as the truth has been revealed," Poppa added.

"Yes, Poppa, such joy in the truth, but again, we are not done." Everyone stopped to look at Nikola. Everyone knew what was next.

CHAPTER 52

"THE REAL FATHER"

"How are we ever going to get those guys to get tested when we don't even know if they will talk with us again, Poppa?" Izrael asked the next day at breakfast.

Momma and Poppa had been wondering the same. "We aren't sure, son," Poppa answered. Momma and I have been talking about just that."

"I wonder if their parents know anything about all of this," Momma said in a hushed thinking out loud tone.

"I doubt it," Iz answered flatly. "Those guys never seemed to be very close to their families."

Hesitantly, adding, "Maybe I will ride over to Cliff's tomorrow" his voice trailing off.

"In the meantime, I would like to talk with Carolina again," Momma said. "I will invite her over and let the girls be here. Nikola has such a soft spot for Jane Mae. She and Josephina can play with Jane Mae while I talk with Carolina."

"It sounds like we have a plan. Let's see what happens then go from there." Poppa stood, nodded to Izrael and the two went out the door to work.

As the day went on, Iz felt the anxiety within him begin to build. Izrael was more familiar with how anxiety started from deep inside him. It began as a burning sensation inside his stomach, moving quickly up through his chest, rushing into his cheeks, followed by a rapid feeling of heat that often left him sweating. While he had learned what to expect, he desperately wanted to learn how to control it. He thought of Momma's words about anxiety and depression. Healing would come later, much later.

Izrael then wondered to himself how things could have changed so much with the Four Musketeers. Such a great team they were. Why would they let a girl like Carolina break up their friendship? It was very disturbing to Iz. He felt his heart breaking knowing he was on his own now, and the ex-friends were now the Three Musketeers. "Those three have a lot in common!" Izrael bluntly said out loud.

Over the next few days Momma made multiple attempts to invite Carolina and Jane Mae over for tea and biscuits. Carolina made several excuses not to go until one day when Mrs. Parker overhead Carolina turning down another invitation.

"What's the matter with you, child?" Mrs. Parker demanded. "The only reason we have gotten through the last several years was from the kindness of that family. Now you talk with Mrs. Kammer again. We will go see them together. We will take Jane Mae with us and make sure they feel good and sorry for us. Be sure to wear your oldest skirt and have Jane Mae dress the same."

"Yes, Ma'am," was Carolina's reluctant reply.

The following day Mrs. Parker, Carolina and Jane Mae arrived at Kammer Ranch for afternoon tea. Suzanah asked her older daughters to join them and help with the preparations.

Everything was beautiful. The table was set as if they were expecting the Queen of England, her daughter and granddaughter. Suzanah never failed to give her all to any and all guests in her home.

After everyone settled in and enjoyed tea and various special cookies, not to mention Suzanah's biscuits along with her homemade jam, the mood around the table changed.

Suzanah began the discussion. She started by explaining the visits and conversations the family had with Izrael's friends. Carolina clearly was feeling uncomfortable. She squirmed and moved her chair forward and backward multiple times while Suzanah spoke. Mrs. Parker loudly interrupted every time with a "SSHHH, stop all that squirming, Carolina!" until Carolina finally let out a squeal like the Kammer family had never heard before. She jumped to her feet, grabbed Jane Mae's left hand, and rushed out the front door.

Suzanah, Lucy and Priscilla all turned towards Mrs. Parker who remained eerily calm. In fact, she was looking down at her fingernails, rotating each hand slightly as she quietly commented on needing to trim her nails.

"Do you want me to go talk with Carolina, Mrs. Parker?" Suzanah somehow managed to say although having much different thoughts she kept to herself.

"She'll be back," Mrs. Parker calmly answered while continuing to study her hands. "She thinks she has to be overly dramatic about everything!" she added while her voice became louder. "That child would scream at a woodpecker if it was bothering her!"

The silence that followed made Lucy and Priscilla uncomfortable. Priscilla stood up and stepped to the stove to begin to reheat the kettle when another loud squeal came from the front porch. Priscilla nearly threw the kettle across the kitchen although somehow managed to set it back down on the stove. She hurried back to the table.

No one said a word.

Within seconds Carolina was back in the kitchen without Jane Mae.

It was Suzanah who asked if Jane Mae was okay.

"She's fine. She's playing," was all Carolina answered.

Nikola and Josephina heard the squealing and hurried to the porch, to attempt to play with Jane Mae again.

After another round of silence, finally Carolina spoke: "There is no way in hell any of those boys will ever be Jane Mae's father!"

"Oh my gosh, Carolina, you are such a dramatic child yourself! Now think really hard about what you are saying, you hear me?" Mrs. Parker said flatly to her only child. "This may be your one chance to keep Jane Mae from being an illegitimate child all her life, are you sure you want to do that?"

"Yes, ma'am, I am sure," Carolina answered flatly then continued, "Those boys did things to me that do not give them any kind of claim to me or my daughter! I will never forgive them, and I refuse to ever tell Jane Mae that story, EVER! She can NEVER know the truth; you all hear me?" Carolina turned, looking directly at each lady around the table as she slowly said her words. "You must promise me!" Carolina added stressing emphasis on "must" in a loud almost growling tone.

Carolina looked back towards Mrs. Parker continuing her low deep tone, "Will you go with me to the courthouse tomorrow? I want to change that stupid birth certificate!"

"You what?" Mrs. Parker managed to answer with a confused look on her face.

"Mrs. Kammer and all of you other Kammer women," Carolina said bluntly and with no emotion, "From now on Jane Mae will be known as Jane Mae Parker with the birth certificate noting father as UNKNOWN, GOT IT?" Carolina's voice grew louder as she finished her last statement, stressing each word, "I will NEVER confess who the real father is!"

Lucy grabbed Priscilla's hand, nearly shivering in unison.

The next deafening silence that followed carried echoes of Carolina's last words in Suzanah's ears. Her heart was racing and breaking at the same time. The pain she felt for Jane Mae, as difficult of a child as she had always been, grew stronger. Suzanah felt much sorrow for her now.

Teatime was over.

Later, during dinner, Momma explained to the rest of the family, "Yes, ultimately Carolina refuses to allow Jane Mae to know the truth of how she was conceived. She demanded we are never allowed to tell Jane Mae the truth, at any time in her life, even when she is grown."

"Why would she say all that, Momma?" Josephina asked. Nikola sat silently but nodded in agreement.

"Carolina pushed and pushed until each of us there agreed to keep her secret. She even demanded her own mother promise not to ever tell the truth to Jane Mae. It was very sad," Momma said in her own sad tone.

The stress of the secret sat heavy on Suzanah and all the family. Nikola hid the heartbreak she felt inside for Jane Mae.

Suzanah did not share what Carolina said in regard to changing the birth certificate. She felt a strong uneasy feeling, unable to shake the suspicion Carolina had no intention of changing it. For now, she, Lucy and Priscilla agreed, not to talk about it again.

Over the next weeks and months the Kammer family naturally pulled further away from Carolina and Jane Mae.

Cliff and Benji deliberately kept their distance from Izrael and all of the Kammer family. MJ also stayed away. In fact, it was as if the three disappeared from the earth, sucked up by lies and secrets, never to be seen again in the beautiful mountain valley they all called home.

CHAPTER 53

"DEAR GRANDMA K"

Izrael wrote to Grandma K just as he had promised he would. Izrael took pride in never breaking his promises. He knew he could find his soul and clear his mind by writing to his grandmother. He went deep Into the Canyon, sat on his favorite large boulder, and began to write:

"DEAR GRANDMA K,

AS PROMISED, I AM WRITING TO SHARE WHAT HAS TAKEN PLACE HERE OVER THE LAST FEW WEEKS. SO MUCH HAS HAPPENED, I AM NOT SURE WHERE TO START.

Izrael described the events that had taken place since he last saw Grandma K and Aunt K, being sure not to include certain parts of the story he was not comfortable sharing.

He continued.

THE GOOD NEWS IN ALL
OF THIS IS THAT THE
FEELING OF GLOOM I SHARED
WITH YOU IS GONE, AND
THE FEAR AROUND BABY
BRIELLA'S BEAUTY HAS BEEN
LIFTED THROUGH MUCH
ANSWERED PRAYER.

MY DEAR GRANDMA K, WE ALL
REALLY TRIED TO HELP THEM.

IT TURNED OUT THERE WAS
NOTHING ELSE WE COULD DO
FOR CAROLINA AND JANE MAE.
THEY STILL LIVE HERE IN
THE VALLEY, BUT I DON'T SEE
THEM MUCH. NIKOLA GOES TO
VISIT AND PLAY WITH JANE
MAE NOW AND THEN. THERE
IS SO MUCH SWEETNESS IN
MY LITTLE SISTER, AS YOU
WELL KNOW.

AS I CLOSE MY LETTER TO
YOU, GRANDMA K, I AM LIS-
TENING TO A NEARBY WOOD-
PECKER. HIS PERSISTENCE
CONTINUES, KNOCKING,
ALWAYS KNOCKING. HE
ALMOST SEEMS TO BE TRYING

TO SEND ME A MESSAGE. I DON'T KNOW WHAT IT IS YET, BUT I KNOW HE WILL NEVER BE GONE. I WAIT FOR HIS MESSAGE TO COME ONE DAY.

I HOPE THAT YOU AND AUNT K ARE DOING WELL. I LOVE AND MISS YOU BOTH SO MUCH.

YOUR GRANDSON,
IZRAEL SHANE KAMMER"

CHAPTER 54

"SHINING IN THE DISTANCE"

After Izrael finished his letter to Grandma K, he pulled out his journal. His thoughts wandered back to the day he found Grandpa K's journal buried. He was not far from the location where he found it, buried in the cold hard clay.

Izrael began to write.

He included a little of what he wrote to Grandma K. Then he confessed to his journal, as he never had done before, how angry and hurt he felt, even going so far as to write the following words angrily and forcefully in an almost messy scribble:

> "I WILL NEVER FORGIVE THEM! SOME THINGS ARE NOT MEANT TO BE FORGIVEN. THE WAY THEY LIED AND KEPT SUCH DARK SECRETS ABOUT CAROLINA AND JANE MAE DISGUSTS ME. I HOPE I NEVER SEE THEM AGAIN AND IF I DO,

I VOW TO NEVER SPEAK TO ANY OF THEM EVER AGAIN! I DON'T FEEL CLOSE TO MY EX-BEST FRIEND, MARCUS JOE, OR MJ, AS WE ALL CALLED HIM, BACK WHEN HE WAS MY FRIEND. HE KEPT SECRETS FROM ME! ALL OF THEM DID! MJ, BENJI, CLIFF, WE HAD SO MUCH FUN IN HIGH SCHOOL BUT THAT IS FAR, FAR BEHIND US NOW. THINGS WILL NEVER BE THE SAME. I WILL NEVER LET ANY OF THEM BACK INTO MY LIFE. NEVER! THIS, I VOW FOREVER!"

After Izrael finished pouring his pain onto the parchment paper, he realized there was one blank sheet left in the journal. He stared down at the page, as if waiting for it to detach itself and fly off into the sky. Izrael then remembered his dream and Momma's interpretation. It all made sense now. He wrote on the last page, a few words about the dream.

THE DREAM, THE LITTLE GIRL RUNNING AWAY. SHE NO LONGER RUNS. SHE IS FREE FROM THE CURSE.

Izrael now knew the little girl was Briella Suzanah Cleveland. The fear that made her run in his dream had lifted. She was safe. No more drama and trouble from Carolina or poor little Jane Mae.

Izrael then heard a tapping sound. He looked up to see a woodpecker pecking on a low branch above his head.

The woodpecker pecked harder and harder, then rapidly flitted from side to side until landing in one spot. He did not give up, persistently, so very persistently, he pecked away at the tree branch. Izrael wondered if the woodpecker was angry.

At that very moment he sensed a message from the woodpecker. A message to never give up. To peck away at the past and release his anger.

He looked down at his journal. He wrote more on the last page, this time about MJ. His suspicions about MJ must have been right. He was sure now why MJ went after Benji like he did that afternoon in the barn. Benji was about to spill MJ's secret. His secret about Carolina and all that he did to her. Izrael's rage grew stronger. He wrote fast and hard as if he were yelling at the top of his lungs.

> "I KNOW WHAT MJ SAID NOW! HE TOLD BENJI, "DON'T SAY IT!" MJ LIED ALL ALONG! HE IS JANE MAE'S FATHER!"

Izrael jumped up and hurried over to Mindee, pulled his knapsack down, reached in and grabbed his small shovel.

He began digging fiercely, using each force into the hard clay to release his hurt and anger. He envisioned his resemblance to the woodpecker. Digging and digging, tapping, and tapping, with fierce persistence.

Persistently, so very persistently.

Izrael wanted his journal to be buried deeper than Grandpa K's journal had been buried. He did not want any of the secrets about Carolina and Jane Mae to ever be found or uncovered by anyone in future generations, especially about MJ being Jane Mae's father. None of them deserved to know the truth. It would be his revenge for all they put him and his family through.

Finally, Izrael fell, exhausted, down on the clay. He strained to prop himself up on his knees. With sweat pouring down the sides of his head and tears streaming down the front of his face, Izrael Shane Kammer blurted out the following words.

"THERE! CAROLINA, JANE MAE, CLIFF, BENJI, AND MJ! I'M DONE WITH ALL OF YOU! NO MORE WILL I LIVE WITH THE DRAMA AND THE LIES YOU ALL CAUSED IN MY LIFE AND THE LIVES OF MY FAMILY!"

"AND NEVER AGAIN WILL THERE BE FOUR MUSKETEERS!"

As the echo of his words bounced across the canyon, Izrael shoved the journal with all his might, down, far, far into the very deep hole he had dug.

He stood to his feet, breathing hard, sweating profusely, still full of emotion. He had never felt this kind of emotion before, and it became loud, so loud he could hear his echo chasing him at the same time he yelled.

He screamed as loud as he had left in his exhausted state.

"I GET IT GRANDMA K! FINALLY I GET IT!"

"THIS COWBOY HAS CLEARED HIS HEART AND MIND OF ALL OF THEM! I HAVE FOUND MY TRUE SOUL, RIGHT HERE, IN THE VERY CENTER OF KAMMER RANCH!!"

Izrael dropped to his knees, his head hanging low. He prayed in a low, scattered, mumbling, groaning voice only God could understand, thanking Him for answering his prayers.

He stood once again, this time tall and proud, as he let his eyes focus hard on everything he could see, across the beautiful Kammer Ranch property. He yelled out one last time. The emotion that was growing inside him blew fast out of his lungs.

"THIS LAND WILL BE ALL MINE ONE DAY! ONLY MINE!"

"NO ONE WILL EVER GET BETWEEN ME AND KAMMER RANCH EVER AGAIN!"

That very afternoon Izrael Shane Kammer, with a fierce determination he had never known before, buried his anger and bitterness deep in the cold hard clay – his own journal, that would never be found, shining, far in the distance, in the center of Kammer Ranch.

"THE COWBOY"

THE COWBOY STRADDLES
HORSES AND WEARS A
BIG SOMBRERO,

SHOOTS IT OUT WITH OUTLAWS
AND THE MEXICAN VAQUERO

THE TOUGH GUY RIDES
THE RANGES AND PACKS A
HEAVY GUN,

SINGS TO HORSE AND
CATTLE AS HE RIDES
BENEATH THE SUN

AT NIGHT WHEN WORK IS
DONE, HE THROWS A BEDROLL
IN THE CLAY,

HIS PISTOL IN ITS HOL-
STER, HOPES TO MAKE IT
ONE MORE DAY

MY PAW-PAW WROTE THAT
POEM, ABOUT THE COWBOY
FROM THE NORTH

THE YOUNG MAN WAS
INSPIRED, BACK IN '44

SCRIBBLED ON OLD PARCH-
MENT, BY A 2:00 A.M.
NIGHTLIGHT

KEROSENE OIL LAN-
TERN TRAINS A COWBOY'S
POINT OF SIGHT

OH THE COWBOY, THE
COWBOY, THE COWBOY IN ME....
THE COWBOY....

Words and Music: Victor O. Medina and grandson, Christopher J. Baker

ABOUT THE AUTHOR

I have been writing this story since I was a little girl, playing with my sister and brother, on the beautiful ranch our father grew up on and took care of throughout his life. I remember sitting on a big boulder, on the hillside, looking down at the house and property and dreaming of one day sharing it with my future family.

I was born in the closest town (with a hospital) to this ranch and spent just a few months of my life living on the ranch, before my parents moved for an improved livelihood. We never stopped going to the ranch on vacations and the very best of my childhood memories were from those vacations. It became our second home. The memories still echo through the trees and "Into the Canyon" of this mountain property.

Most of my life has been living in Albuquerque, New Mexico, where my husband, Vernon, and I live now. We share a love of the mountains and hope to ultimately retire in the northern New Mexico community which inspired this book.

Our greatest enjoyment comes from spending time with our grown children and grand girls.

My love of writing is where this trilogy started, many years ago, when it felt mostly like a place to be creative. The fact that it turned into a true novel takes my breath away. God's hand is all over it, as I could never have done this without Him leading me, page after page. I pray it sparks memories of your own and brings you enjoyment as you read.

FURTHER READINGS

"Into the Canyon" - the first in the trilogy of the Kammer Family.

The final book in the trilogy to be released in late 2025.

www.ingramcontent.com/pod-product-compliance
Lightning Source LLC
Jackson TN
JSHW020927270125
77800JS00002B/5
9798868508776